THE FUNK SONATRA PROJECT

An Epic Sci-Fi Novella

O.W. SERELLUS

MYND MATTERS

Mynd Matters Publishing
715 Peachtree Street NE, Suites 100 & 200
Atlanta, GA 30308
www.myndmatterspublishing.com

978-1-948145-54-1 (pbk)
978-1-948145-55-8 (ebook)

FIRST EDITION

To my lovely wife, Joanne Williams,
and my three daughters, Mahal, Fela, Najah

CONTENTS

THE FUNK SONATRA PROJECT

CHAPTER ONE

THE RACE IS ABOUT TO BEGIN

Adorn yourself in a sleek pair of Ray-Bans, a striking Formula 500 jacket, a crisp pair of charcoal Levi's, and an attitude both fearless and humble all at once. What you have is *Ultimate Cool*. Likewise, if you possess a sexy, velvet voice that can hold its own against any vocalist that was, is, and is yet to come, that's pretty cool too. In either case, if you're sporting timeless style, a great smile, and winning personality, *Ultimate Cool* is definitely your name and game. Hardly anyone ever achieves *Ultimate Cool*. Ever. Let alone for most of a lifetime.

But it *is* a cool 2010 and the drag race culture in northern California is hot, heavy, and happening. An up-and-coming driver is celebrated for his unconquerable driving prowess and of course, for his cool. Rok is good-looking with swag on ten. He's a walking throwback mix of 1950s cool infused with 1970s soul. With love and appreciation for all things harmonious, his selection of music while drag racing is designated, "The Frank Sinatra Jazz Genre." Other drivers are rightfully confused and cannot comprehend why a new urban legend (and sometimes church drummer and bass player) would listen to such old, "has-been" music while doing what he does best. But one person's confusion is another's passion and ethos!

For remember, it is not about youthfulness or era, it's all about cool and achieving the *Ultimate Cool*. Timeless and transcendent. One thing Rok is, is cool. In fact, he epitomizes cool. Racing the masses on and off the blacktop. Winning, but in competition with no one. Just like his idol whose tunes he relishes, Francis Albert Sinatra. A decent musician himself, Rok totally digs Frank's vibes. There's something about the Chairman of the Board singing "Come Fly with Me" and "Fly Me to the Moon (In Other Words)" that really gets Rok flying down the track, winning race after race. That *something* of course has to be filed under *Ultimate Cool*. Difficult to explain or define, but definitely something Rok knew Frank understood and possessed.

So, after enjoying another winning night at the

drag races, Rok heads home. As he comes to a halt at a stoplight, he pauses to adjust his shades. Fog envelops the night's sky. A snazzy, blue Porsche glides up and stops at the intersection beside him. Recognizing each other, Rok knows the driver is untested and eager to demonstrate his mettle. Rok, a legend in his time, remains unbeaten and the best driver on all the tracks throughout northern California. Hell, pretty much throughout the whole state. Anxious for a confrontation, the driver of the Porsche begins instigating a race between them by aggressively revving his engine. With a wry grin, he yells to Rok, "Pinks! Let's race for pinks, chump!"

Rok glances over and smiles indifferently at the rookie. Reluctantly, he turns down the funky album blasting through his speakers. He had been digging that sound.

"I don't have any of my racing music and I don't really want to race without it," he replies.

A coupla hours earlier he had traded a choice Frank Sinatra CD for the funky sounds now playing through his car stereo. Considering his current situation, it may not have been a smart move on his part. A kid was trying to peddle his demo to Rok and begged him to listen. Rok had agreed but only if the kid promised to give Sinatra a chance. The kid jumped at the opportunity to have his beats blast through Rok's sound system.

The Porsche's driver gestures and Rok knows they are to strike off when the light turns green. Having never been one to decline a challenge, Rok smiles, shrugs, and says, "Why not?"

However, this will be the first time he'll be racing without listening to Ol' Blue Eyes' perfect voice.

"Man, oh man," he mutters to himself. "The Chairman helps me loosen up when I race. This will be interesting...and tight!" In fact, Sinatra's music enables Rok to take his street drag racing skills to a higher level of performance and success, a level that few, if any, have ever achieved. The *Ultimate Cool*.

Seconds before the light turns green, Rok decides on a change of music to vibe to while racing the rookie driver. It is a decision destined to alter the course of his life and forever change the world of music.

CHAPTER TWO

POINT OF NO RETURN

He's in a coma lying on a steel-framed bed in a cold, sterile hospital room. While yet unconscious and unable to express his awareness, he hears the name "Officer Whitely," followed by an official-sounding voice discussing details of a violent automobile accident. Rok heeds his name being spoken as the litany of injuries suffered from the crash are discussed. Then, there are words painfully describing the careless driving of a certain judge's son. The young, reckless, privileged fool had caused the crash, facilitating his own death. Rok drifts back off into a deep sleep.

***

Sometime later, it could have been days or weeks, Rok finds himself still unable to see or speak, existing in a virtual prison, a coma arresting his consciousness. Somehow, he is still cognizant of his surroundings and listens as people identified as Dr. Billis and Nurse LaRue, discuss his current condition and dire prognosis. Offhandedly, they comment on the devil-may-care behavior of young, irresponsible kids foolishly given license to drive and race fast cars on dangerous curves, and how this senseless accident could have been so easily averted.

In a slow progression, familiar strains of beauty filter into his cloudy thoughts. His favorite music plays. Ol' Blues Eyes himself. Emanating in the unfiltered realm of his unconscious mind. Like a dream within a dream, it's barely audible, and suspending him in his semi-conscious state. Adjacent to the faint resonance of Sinatra singing, "I've Got You Under My Skin," Rok detects and recognizes the night janitor cleaning his room.

"Skinny" is fully aware of Rok's medical condition, Rok knows this. The janitor often talks to him while cleaning the items within the four walls, never expecting a response. Sometimes he just visits. It seems like years have passed since the old janitor began reading the daily paper to him, keeping him abreast of each day's happenings. During his visits, he always turns on some light jazz or funk from an old mp3 player he carries while going about his daily tasks.

Rok's reputation as a drag racer preceded him to the intensive care unit long before the accident that found him comatose. There is a camaraderie in the old man's voice. A quiet, unassuming affinity for him that Rok can't quite understand but nonetheless, appreciates. They all hope for his survival and resurrection from the coma in which he dwells. However, Rok is uncertain which of them really cares more. His own voice is silent on the matter and can provide no clarity to his partial indifference. His frustration and determination have given way to apathy.

Two months pass and an air evacuation unit arrives to transport Rok and his small bag of belongings to a state-of-the-art clinic just outside the city limits of San Francisco for a breakthrough, experimental treatment. The crew expertly load him onto the rotary-winged aircraft. Careful not to cause further injury, they secure his bed and shout a few commands over the sounds of the turbo-shaft engines and gravity-defying rotors. A gust of hot air engulfs Rok as they begin their ascent.

Mere moments into the flight, he feels the once steady aircraft tremble, its weight shifting from side to side. Rok hears the desperate, panicked voices of the crew and the sounds of control panel alarms warning of impending doom. There's a problem! They have flown into a rapidly-forming thunderstorm undetected by radar. The pilot targets the eye of the storm as bolts of lightning slash and narrowly miss striking the aircraft. Seconds later, a powerful thunderclap consumes the scene, its reverberations intense and frightening. Sheets of blinding electrical light flash. An engine fails along with the rear rotors. A second engine unsuccessfully struggles to maintain power as the chopper spins out of control. Suddenly, there is calm and the revolutions cease. It is a moment of eerie silence as the aircraft is suspended in mid-air within the eye of the storm, while lightning and thunder consume the body of the storm.

For a time, the machine hangs pendulously in midflight. Then a strange, inexplicable event occurs. Both the lightning and thunder abruptly cease and the aircraft is overcome by darkness. It's pitch black. The iron bird drops toward the earth. Those inside the helicopter are helpless to stop its sudden, swift descent, and brace themselves in hopeless, gripping terror. The plane meets the ground in an intense confrontation. The pilot, copilot, and two medical personnel are killed instantly, their bodies strewn among the fiery wreckage. But there is one lone survivor, Rok! Tossed a safe distance from the burning helicopter and no longer strapped to the gurney, Rok not only finds himself safe and unharmed, but awake and fully conscious. Miraculously, what one violent accident has effected, a second and even more terrible disaster has undone!

Dressed in the very same clothing worn the night of his street-racing accident, Rok's limbs tingle as the sensation returns to his arms and legs. He manages to crawl farther away from the mangled, burning metal indicating the scene of impact. The helicopter rests in the middle of what appears to be acres of lush vineyards. Enormous grapes the size of soccer balls have apparently absorbed much of the force of the crash. He attempts to process it all, but his senses are overwhelmed. He is overcome by awe and amazement. Dizzy and disoriented, Rok blacks out.

CHAPTER THREE

REVVING BACK UP

Time, again, holds no meaning for Rok. How much of it has or hasn't passed, he doesn't consider. When he regains consciousness and examines his surroundings, he finds himself on another sheeted bed within another white-washed room.

One thing is immediately and annoyingly clear to him, someone has horrible taste in music! The cacophony of infuriating noise blasting from outside the open door to his room agitates him. It is the worst arrangement of "rhythmic" sounds his ears have ever suffered. Within seconds, he feels the onset of a migraine. The rebellious pulse in his temples throbs in tempo to the oppressive tune flooding his space.

Fully awake and still dressed in his original street clothes, he spots his shoes on a nearby chair. Without difficulty, he ambles out of bed, retrieves the shoes, and secures them to his feet. He wiggles his toes for good measure. He's feeling mighty agile and it strikes him as odd that he feels no pain. He's definitely fully awake and no longer in a coma. A sense of wholeness overtakes him. Wait, there's his gym bag, the one he had with him in his car a few days ago. Or was it months ago? He's not sure but it doesn't matter. There's his bag, the door is wide open, and he's got his legs back. Time to step out and "put on the Ritz!"

As soon as he walks out of the room, his ears ache. The piercing racket is resoundingly louder in the hallway. Except for the noise, Rok is more than ready for a long walk. He could use it. He heads down the narrow hallway, passing closed doors on either side. *Someone's got to turn off this awful music,* he thinks to himself. *I will do it myself if need be!* In fact, he approaches the room where this need is ready to be fulfilled. In the center stands a lanky, dark-haired kid around thirteen or fourteen years old, dressed in a plaid t-shirt and skinny, ripped jeans, rocking his head back and forth in time to the discordant music. His eyes are closed. He's in his zone.

"Hey!" Rok screams. "Give it a rest!"

The startled kid opens his eyes and blinks a few times, surprised to find Rok across from him. Without missing a beat, the kid grabs a sophisticated looking remote control, aims it at the nearby boom box, and mutes the noise. The scene is surreal to Rok as he makes eye contact with the shaggy-haired youth.

"Thanks! Silence can be fun. Now, where am I?" Rok asks, allowing his voice to soften.

Grinning, the teenager answers, "The real question is, *who* are you! But what the hell man, are you all right? I mean, what's with that crunched-up plane we found you at in the fields?"

He looks at Rok with a friendly, concerned smile filled with continuing inquiry. The kid had never seen anyone like Rok. His father had told him stories of people like him before, but he had never seen one in person. His dark skin looked smooth and his hair was fluffy like the stuff in pillows. He wanted to touch it but dared not.

"Well? What's up with that fit you wearing?" Noticing Rok's confusion, he laughs.

"My name is Pooky. What's yours?"

"Rok, nice to meet ya," Rok quietly answers. Then, shaking his head he asks, "What are you doing with a name like Pooky? Do you know where that name comes from?"

"Yep, sure I know. My dad named me after a guy

he knew from Gotham. But that's my name just the same!"

Rok just grins. At least his migraine is going away.

"That's a strange name for a kid like you, you know. A guy from Gotham, huh? Rok pauses for a moment but decides it's better not to ask for details.

"By the way, where *are* your parents?"

"It's just me and my pops and our farm here. But hey, you don't like my name and clothes, okay, that's cool. I'm just being me, ya know. But what you got against my beats? I mean, you *have* heard of POP-BANG techno-music, right?"

"Nooo, I can't say that I have," Rok answers slowly.

"Well, it's exactly how it sounds. POP-BANG! Be from the streets! Ya pop or bang against your neighbor, ya teacher, whoever. Anybody can get it!"

The kid's arms flail as he speaks, reminding Rok of the air dancers he'd see bringing attention to car lots as he cruised down the boulevard.

"Wow kid, are you all right?" Rok somewhat smirks, "Why you so into being violent? What's with that music?"

"I'm not violent. I'm just preaching what's playing. It ain't my style, really. I just be holler'n."

Rok surmises that Pooky is the most innocuous-looking teenager he's ever laid eyes upon. Mild-mannered and docile come to mind. A direct juxtaposition to his words. A caricature of sorts.

"Well, you should try to play something else. Something calm and smooth, with melody and rhythms. Anyway, where's your dad?"

"He's outside in the vineyards looking at your aircraft. Evaluating the scene. It's bodies out there man. We don't know how you survived."

"Hmm. What is this aircraft you keep mentioning?" Rok asks dubiously.

"It's right outside. Let's go, I'll show you."

CHAPTER FOUR

THE CREATIVE PROCESS

Meanwhile, on the other side of this same catastrophic continent, an unctuous judge holds court inside the infamous Oval Courtroom. Located at 1600 Pennsylvania Avenue within the Presidential Palace, the Oval Courtroom is filled to capacity this fine, miserable day. These days, the courtrooms are one of the few sources of unfettered entertainment. Unfettered that is, if you don't count the bailiff's half-hearted attempts to restore order when the judge demands. The judge sometimes allows the gallery's insolence to go unchecked as the reactions to the harsh penalties for the slightest of crimes add to the intended effect. Deterrence. Almost all of the desperate, servile onlookers are homeless people and other disenfranchised souls who ravenously populate the Washington, D.C. area—now called WDC—in the year 2083. However, others have been officially summoned to mandatory Gallery Duty, a court-initiated effort to ensure the court remains full of spectators.

It is a large courtroom located in the right-wing of the White House. A cold and austere one at that. Uniformed police officers wearing helmets and armed with electric stock prods surround the rowdy populace seated at benches which encircle the prisoner's cage. Inside the steel cage sits a scruffy looking, meagerly-dressed girl probably no older than fifteen or sixteen years of age. Bruises dot her neck and arms. An expression of dazed fear and abject resignation contort her features. Of the one hundred or so spectators gathered, half look upon her with tired, sympathetic eyes. The other half with hostility and a thirst for blood.

"Order! Order in the court!" commands a flabby, slack-jawed, bald-headed man from his seated perch behind the glinting steel-encased bench overlooking the spacious, dingey courtroom. He is Judge Whitely, Justice of The Unpeace, for it not justice or peace sought or litigated in his chambers. But the unpeace of ruthless law and power. His own, and that of his supreme ruler and master, Da Man.

Slamming down his mallet-sized gavel thrice more to quiet the boisterous onlookers and restore order, he gestures to the captain of his court guards to assist. The captain merely snaps his fingers and several of his helmeted guards remove their stock prods and begin shocking those assembled in the front pews of the courtroom. Snapping his fingers once more, the captain's men return their weapons in unison and resume parade rest before the now cowed assemblage. Instantly, an eerie silence ensues.

"That's what I'm talkin' about!" snickers the judge. "Order and discipline. Law and power will be the rule. Is that understood?"

In one voice, with the captain and his enforcement guards, the whole throng of hostile, impoverished-looking people answer.

"Yes, your honor!"

"Excellent. Then we will continue with the verdict unless anyone has an objection."

Whitely is met with silence and down-turned heads from the pacified and subdued members of the gallery.

"Very well," he slightly more than whispers. "Will the defendant please rise and face the court?"

The young, frightened girl struggles to her feet, then slowly turns to face Judge Whitely, despite the iron shackles pressing against her ankles and shins.

"You are guilty of attempting to funk against the law. Penal Code 12-1234. An act of being a creative musician. You know it's against the New World Order Law. Do you know you are not to be creative? Do you know what kind of crime you commit if you attempt to do this? For your crime, you will serve your time in the Ignoritis Machine. You will learn how to develop ignorant experiences and habits. You will learn total subservience. You will learn to blindly hate those who go against the majority and vote for whoever promises a chicken in your pot. There are a number of things you'll learn that will lead to long-term failure. Most importantly, you are to create nothing of value. Nothing of excellence. If anything is to be created, we, the World Wide Order, will create it! In this case, our music, our literature, our media. Mediocre tunes and Pop-Bang Music are those on which you will exist. For we command you to create nothing. Creativity is eschewed! Court adjourned. Everyone is dismissed!"

Immediately, two muscular court guards unlock the cage and drag the convicted girl to a side door and hastily from the courtroom. The crowd of faceless observers and drowsy participants seems kowtowed and indifferent as they slowly usher themselves out of the arena in which they had sought entertainment.

Through a rear door a few steps down from his presiding bench, Whitely squeezes his ponderous frame and steps into an adjoining antechamber and long hallway. Holding his judge's robes so as not to trip over them, he ungracefully strolls to a waiting elevator. Once inside, after the elevator doors shut, he gazes into a retina scanner near the front of the lift. Within seconds, an ominous red light scans his eyes. A second later, the elevator quickly descends.

Down several floors it plummets while Whitely stands rigidly inside, almost in a trance, patiently waiting to reach the elevator's subterranean destination. At last, the location display reads S-30, and the elevator comes to an abrupt halt. Again, Whitely gathers his loose robes in hand, and effortlessly turns the slight twinge of fear spouting his face into one of false, forced warmth and greeting. In that moment, the doors fly open, and he prepares to briskly step out.

Before him stands a hulking man, his head and body covered by a dark blue cape and hood, his swarthy metallic features hidden in the recess of shadow. He reaches out with a large pewter hand to welcome Whitely off the lift and into the spacious underground apartment which the giant calls home, office, and sanctuary.

"A job well done, my servant. Soon, there will be no more creative musicians left in the world to annoy us and every person on Earth will listen to what I program. No more funk, jazz, rock, pop, classical, or hip-hop music. No more soulful singing or R&B. Good-bye melodic music, harmonious music and meaningful words, or emotional entreaty. Nothing innovative. Then, no more redeeming art in any form. All creativity will be banned and I will assume total control. With the president in my pocket, no one can stop me."

The judge smiles respectfully at the formidable man who has spoken and who has waited so patiently to welcome him from his difficult task on the surface above. How kind of his benefactor to personally greet him! Whitely knows him too well. He has to be gracious at such a time. His leader and patron is to be thanked as well as obeyed. And of course, always feared. He is Da Man.

Da Man, whose sinister voice announces to all and reminds them without exception, that every individual must obey the New World Order Law. Disobey and a fate worse than death awaits. For Da Man is the master of order and the purveyor of law and power. He, Judge

Whitely, is his first lieutenant and most servile beneficiary. Whitely knows Da Man as none other ever will. He knows his lofty goal is to own and control all entertainment entities as well as run and operate most of the puppet government. What he says, goes.

If you want to produce a movie, paint a picture, record an album, or do anything artistic, you need Da Man's permission. The most malevolent thing about Da Man, other than his grotesque six-foot-nine physicality and brutal proclivities, is one can only create under his rules and his system. Those who do so are financially rewarded. But only after one has completely sworn one's self over to Da Man in body and spirit. Total servitude is required. Total worship of Da Man is paramount for existence and the noble purpose is to be attained.

You see, Da Man has a noble agenda. It is engineered for the greater good and everyone's personal welfare and safety. It's an agenda to eliminate true creativity, literally, to squash as one would, an insect. All creative people and independent thought must be regulated. But this is to keep people free and alive and well, of course.

Because he is Da Man. Therefore, he knows creativity must be totally eradicated and wiped from the face of the earth. Its existence is an anathema to his own and to the power and control he wields and needs in order to progress. In order to keep providing for the common good. Creativity, innovation, and ingenuity are the worst of all freedoms. It is what allows people to open their minds and think. To hope, to dream, to aspire, to be brave, to believe in goodness and morality, and to produce and become better. Creativity leads to the practice of individualism and for people to freely express themselves. Such freedom, as only Da Man knows too well, is what leads to resistance and rebellion and would, eventually, lead to his own downfall and demise. Creativity leads to free thought, free will, and inspiration! This, of course, is unacceptable. People must not be allowed to be inspired. That leads to thinking and dreaming, which become hope and finally, rebellion.

Unctuous, servile, and ever ready to please, Judge Whitely knows the nonsensical palaver only too well. As if the words were his very own. But his master is a man of brutal muscle, ruthless will, and eloquent words. He, Judge Whitely, is only a flabby follower and poor imitation of ruthlessness whose greatest claim to power is mouthing brutality taught and controlled by another—his master, Da Man. Who, he reminds himself, can be easy to work for when you remember the importance of servility.

However, in another corner of the globe, something of equal importance needs to be examined.

CHAPTER FIVE

WU-KILLERS, INC.

Somewhere in the darkest regions of South America, the New Co-op China's top covert investment firm and the C.I.A operate Wu-Killers, Incorporated, a joint training center. Its *clan*destine mission is teaching select women to be covert killers and superlative assassins. The women are the modern-day embodiment of the Amazonian single-breasted warrioresses, and the feared and fabled Japanese Onna-bugeisha. By the time a graduate finishes the program, she will have become an expert sharpshooter, certified on every firearm in the world's arsenal.

The school also calls for a strenuous training regimen which consists of mud wrestling de-clawed, semi-muzzled bears and engaging in simulated interactive fights with the famous Bruce Lee and

Muhammad Ali software programs. In addition, the cadets master underwater tai chi and kung fu, training twice daily in a pool for three-hour sessions wearing heavy scuba gear. Along with other exhaustive and lethal forms of combat, assassination techniques, and rigorous training, they learn and repeatedly practice until the ability to exterminate a target by any means necessary becomes second nature.

In this year's class, there is a very special trainee, Agent Nzinga 5000. However, it is not just her outstanding test scores and superior fighting skills that make her desirable to the special interest groups who contract new assassins from Wu-Killers, Inc. She is also the most beautiful warrioress to walk the earth. One who sports, of course, a major attitude! Her supervisors figure the combination of beauty and boldness can achieve any objective and accomplish any goal in any environment. She is the classic "honeypot" redefined for modern warfare. In Agent Nzinga 5000's case, her beauty was recognized early in life. Her overprotective parents sent her to Tibet at age seven. There, she started her martial arts training and became an acolyte of Buddhism.

All this, she accomplished by age twelve, which drew the attention of Wu-Killers, Inc. In time, they persuaded her parents to allow them to provide her with additional training and discipline at their main facility in South America. In return, they agreed to send her to Obama University, the most prestigious university in the world, with her tuition paid in full. As an added incentive, they also provided Nzinga 5000's family with a lavish lifestyle including a luscious, staffed estate and a monthly stipend. But the cost was well worth it. By age twenty-two, Nzinga 5000 was accredited with successfully completing fifty-two missions for the organization. That's fifty-two successful operations of annihilation and assassination worldwide. Wu-Killers, Inc, with its infinite resources, is more than happy to keep Nzinga 5000's large extended family of parents, siblings, cousins, and even third cousins twice removed, living in the lap of luxury.

However, Agent Nzinga 5000 is more than just a killing machine. She is also a person. Her real name is Anna Nzinga LaRue. Her racial ambiguity is not uncommon these days. In fact, some version of the Procreation Act of 2025, which outlaws marriage between two people of the same ethnicity, has been adopted by most countries. Yet, her looks are still striking. In outright defiance of the attempts to create a homogeneous society, her genes betray clear hints of defined ethnicity. Her skin is shades darker than the common tan complexions of her peers. Her long dark locs curl tighter than most. Her almond eyes are those of her father who hails from the Orient. Her mother is Creole. A survivor of Louisiana's Hurricane Katrina some fifty years prior, Ella Lee passed on her survival instincts and savvy to her daughter from the womb. Anna adopted several other salient characteristics from her mom, most notably her tireless willpower, an inability to quit anything, and an extremely sassy, feisty attitude. All of which combine to make her a very attractive assassin.

Finding herself impoverished and alone after the hurricane, Ella Lee traveled to California's Bay Area. Even to this day, she will mention to anyone within earshot how the federal government still won't admit to the miserable relief effort provided to the victims of such a destructive storm.

Anna's father is known for being a kind and loving individual, but woe to anyone who takes his kindness for weakness. He is a ninth level Shoalin gung fu master. His simple name is Kimo, and while working as a volunteer at a homeless shelter in the Bay Area, he met and fell in love with Ella Lee who had been staying at the shelter in the aftermath of the storm. He invited her to his home. After a few months of living together, Kimo and Ella Lee married and exactly nine months later, Anna took her first breath.

CHAPTER SIX

THE DUNGEON OF DA MAN

Underground, beneath the now austere, but historical presidential mansion some thirty stories above, in lush, opulent furnishings, two animated figures engage in a heated conversation.

"Judge Whitely, how is it I'm detecting creative music that has just been produced?" Sitting in an oversized leather chair, with a tinge of raw anger in his voice, Da Man stares across the shiny marble table separating him from his plump house guest. His gaze has its desired effect.

"What?" whimpers Judge Whitely, his voice close to panic. "How can that be? I'll pull up the files right this minute, sir!"

In front of him sits a sleek computer loaded with the latest technology. The judge taps his fingers over the keyboard at lightning speed as if to show Da Man just how diligent a servant he is.

"Well, master, this sudden manifestation seems to be coming from the western part of the country. But wait, look here! Isn't that where...?" his voice trails off as both men glare at the computer screen, their faces frozen in disbelief.

"It can't be. I thought we killed him and his group," Da Man demands. "He must have some sort of force field or maybe a special jammer interfering with our surveillance. Did we not bomb and totally annihilate his base and eliminate the last of the AGCA? That terrorist scum." He spits out the last line in disgust.

"I'm not sure, quivers Judge Whitely.

"Well, it must have been a decoy base. Regardless my servant, you must go now and find a way to decimate him and his elk once and for all. There has to be a way to bypass his systems. Even at its best, his technology should be no match to ours. What can you find?"

After rigorously punching more keys, Whitely turns and frowns at Da Man as he watches his leader's reaction to the sonic beauty that starts playing over the loudspeakers throughout the subterranean vault. It's the sound of really funky funk music. Its soul stirring, emotionally charged rhythms have a hypnotic effect. Lacking willpower, the judge is unable to resist the lilting charms and melodious flow. It moves through his mind and body and he begins tapping his feet and moving his head in sync to the music. A dour, tone-deaf man, the judge's movements are visibly a little off but he's lost in the moment. He feels it to his core and is unable to sit still, much to the chagrin of Da Man.

"Stop that, damn it! You imbecile! Stop before I make you stop...and pay dearly for your rebellious behavior!"

"Yes, my master, I...I'm sorry. It went through me, and...and it felt...well, really good!"

"Enough! I don't want to hear such nonsense. No more of that disgusting sound! Turn it off."

Da Man is beside himself and doesn't try to restrain his infuriation over what he has just witnessed and heard. His face is red with fury and his fists are clinched against his sides as he towers over Whitely, fixing the servile judge in a terrible gaze.

"Go! Now! Find a way to rid me of these loathsome creatures. Immediately! Don't you understand? This threatens my entire cause! I'm on the verge of eliminating all creativity and free thought everywhere! I'm closer than ever so I cannot allow this music to be exposed to the public. Find whoever you need. Take whatever you must. But find them and destroy them. And don't come back until it's finished!"

"Yes, master." With a terror-stricken expression swathing his features, and in a cowering posture, Whitely hurries from the room and to the elevator. He hastily places a call while entering the lift. Important work awaits him in his courthouse office thirty stories above Da Man's creepy subterranean sanctuary. The fresh air will do him some good.

Soon thereafter, safely ensconced in his judge's chambers, and grinning like a sharp-toothed tiger who has just devoured a truckload of chirping minor birds, Whitely sits back, pleased with himself. He has hired Wu-Killers, Inc., the most highly-touted company of assassins in the world, to execute his boss' orders. Ruthless and always unfailing, Wu- Killers, Inc. assured the judge that the contract will be carried out swiftly and with complete success. In fact, they have assigned their best agent to the task. The most lethal lovely assassin the world has ever seen, the one and only, Nzinga 5000. Ha! This funky creative music—which sources have identified as The Funk Sonatra Project— has just seen and played its last funk!

Meanwhile, great things are beginning to happen back at the peaceful, loquacious vineyards…

CHAPTER SEVEN

DAYS OF FUTURE PAST

"You don't know who my pops is?" Pooky inquires as he shows Rok a family portrait.

"No, not really. Who is he?" Rok curiously replies.

"Hs name is Billis Gater, II. He's a pretty powerful dude and his money doesn't hurt. He's one of the last of the AGCA," Pooky proudly explains.

Rok thinks he's heard the name Billis before. "What's the AGCA?"

"Man, oh, man. You've never heard of A Group Creating for All? They've been around since 2025. Where you from, man?" Pooky asks. "By the way, how'd you get past our air cameras?"

"Air cameras? 2025?" Rok stares at Pooky as if seeing him for the first time. He decides the kid must be insane.

"Yeah, we have satellites. They provide live coverage over all our property. The whole estate is two miles long and three miles wide."

"Well, damn!" Rok smiles. "That's a big vineyard. I'm impressed."

"You really don't remember flying over the area, do ya? You didn't see where you were heading before you crashed?"

Rok shakes his head and looks askance, annoyed at himself over his memory lapse.

"All I remember is being in my hot rod at a stoplight, vibing to some funky music. Then some young dude asked me to race him…drag race him right then and there. I think I remember beating him, but I can't recall the details or anything that happened after that. I vaguely remember a hospital, but it's really all a blur."

"If you were racing in a car, then what were you doing in that copter just a few days ago? I remember reading about tanks and copters in my U.S. History class. That's some deep shit, man."

"Yeah, right, kid. Just show me the crash site, okay?"

"Sure, come on."

Outside, near the downed helicopter, Rok and

Pooky stroll about the scene, examining at length the awful wreckage and four decomposing bodies. Rummaging through the aircraft's severed fuselage, they notice emergency decals and EMT equipment, giving clues to the aircraft's use and mission. Covering his nose, Rok can't help but remark, "It stinks around here! Who are these dead people, anyway?"

"They were with you in the crash. When Pops and I carried you to the house yesterday morning, you were out of it. We were surprised you survived," answers Pooky.

"Hmm, well personally, I think I've seen...and smelled enough."

Rok finds himself feeling confused. "I don't know these people. I don't remember them."

He notes that the pilot and copilot are still strapped in their seats, and the mangled bodies of a male paramedic and female nurse lie in separate locations nearby among smaller burnt fragments of the helicopter. They appear to have been dead for at least a day or two, their faces and exposed flesh are swollen and decomposition has set in. In their present state, their faces are unrecognizable.

"So, my bag was with me when you found me?"

"Yep and we didn't open it or look inside, you can

be sure. It should be just as you left it," says Pooky.

Not far from one of the aircraft's side exits, Rok spots a clipboard with sheets of paper still attached. The documents are legible. The papers bear his name, medical data, and history. He can't believe it! His eyes dart rapidly as he scans the paperwork line by line. He learns that he had been in a coma and the helicopter was moving him to a special clinic somewhere just outside the city of San Francisco. He suddenly looks up and gazes across the vineyards at Pooky and the property. In the far horizon, the vague outline of a city's skyline is visible. But it's a pitiful representation of a skyline, with only a handful of separated high-rises dotting the distant landscape.

Pooky stands mystified reading over Rok's shoulder, and notices the date printed on the papers and forms attached to the clipboard. His reaction is quick and uncontrolled.

"What? 2010? You're from 2010? How's that even possible? This is some weird shit going on here."

"What are you talking about?" Rok still feels confused and scowls at Pooky. But he can feel a strange uneasiness building in the pit of his stomach.

"Well, the year today is 2083!" Pooky exclaims while watching Rok in a suspiciously cautious manner, acutely aware his face must look as confused and disturbed as Rok's.

"What? You're kidding me, right?" Rok whispers back. "I can see the skyline of San Francisco there…"

"I think you mean San Franco," Pooky interjects.

"Whatever!" Rok annoyingly responds. "It's not the same. There's hardly anything left of it. Where are all the buildings?" Rok bends over to catch his breath as he feels his chest rise and beads of sweat form on his forehead. This is some freaky shit. The future? 2083? Rok knows how unbelievable it all sounds but can't shake the reality of the moment. Panic settles in.

"Hey, try to relax, okay? Take a look at my watch." Pooky extends his left arm to Rok, displaying the unusual contraption that adorns his wrist. The glowing dials around its large illuminated face remind Rok of a plane's control panel.

At first, Rok stares in amazement, then urgency interrupts his awe.

"Kid, there's got to be real answers here, right? I mean, how is this possible? Wait…what's that? Hold up."

Shaking his head in disbelief, he finds himself entranced by the technical wonderment appearing from Pooky's watch.

"Look," Pooky interjects. After pushing two buttons, he activates a special feature. A three-dimensional scene appears on the watch's surface. Rok passes his fingers through the image. The digital transmission continues without interruption.

They watch as a sharply-dressed newscaster delivers a monologue, detailing significant events occurring across the country.

Twenty-four hour news, Rok thinks. *Some things haven't changed.*

"…and after the Great California off-the-Richter-scale earthquake, the new colony of Lost Angeles is now beginning to see positive growth for its citizens once more. Property value is going up after a forty-five-year plummet. The employment rate, of course, remains high, at 72% now throughout the whole country. The poverty and homelessness rates continue to drop, now boasting 52%. Meanwhile, please make note that the 91st pay-per-view execution is rescheduled for next Friday night. If you planned to attend, previously purchased tickets will remain valid for the new date."

Suddenly, the image of an attractive female newscaster appears.

"We have breaking news. A new candidate has just

been cleared to enter the presidential race. Reagan Kennedy, the white man whose previous attempts to run were marred in scandal, including allegations that he was ineligible due to his ancestry. After facing an uphill legal battle to establish his citizenship, Mr. Kennedy now finds himself in the race. It should be interesting to see. The question remains, is America ready for a president that does not look like her? This could be history folks. The last racially defined president we have seen was in 2016. Now let us return to our regular broadcast…"

"Now watch this," Pooky tells Rok. Speaking to the watch, he commands, "Turn to sports."

Instantly, another newscaster in a different news room occupies the watch's console and is caught mid-sentence delivering news.

"…the best dunk of the year is by Jerry Gomez-Chu out of Williams-Williams University, from two feet over the top of the rim completing a triple somersault reverse dunk!"

Rok stares in fascination as the scene comes alive across the surface of Pooky's watch. A college basketball game is on and an athlete, presumably Jerry Gomez-Chu, is seen stealing the basketball from an opponent from half court. He leaps mid-court and completes his acrobatic feat before stuffing the ball through the net with one hand. Rok's eyes light up, and he feels more uneasy than ever. This is a helluva phenomenon.

Shit has changed! He muses, not sure what to make of the future. The excitement of the game wasn't enough for him to forget the dire statistics recited by the broadcaster. Plus, that thing about a white guy not being able to run for president? Rok took a closer look at Pooky. He had tanned skin, much lighter than his own, but clearly not white. His long, dark hair hung in loose waves down to his shoulders. Rok really hadn't given his race a second thought.

He squints at Pooky. "This is what athletes are doing these days? Damn!"

"Yeah, of course," Pooky deadpans.

"You have 3D TV on your watch! You said you have satellite cameras that observe the air space around here. Can we access them and go see us, you know, me, when I landed here? I mean, crashed here?"

"I don't see why not. Follow me back to the house." Rok shoots one last forlorn look at the destroyed helicopter and its four dead occupants, then hurries to catch up to Pooky as they head toward the futuristic-looking house, complete with striking angles and a dome roof. This time, Rok notices how immense the domicile actually is, and glances back over his shoulder to assess the giant-sized fruit growing in the vineyards. They had previously escaped his scrutiny.

"Man, those grapes in the yard are humongous."

Overhearing Rok, Pooky laughs, "Yeah, we modify them, enhancements you could say. We had to do something for sustainment. After the Carnivore Trials, a lot of farmland was destroyed. It became too much with everyone only eating plant-based food. Farmers couldn't keep up with the demand. We had to come up with ways to grow stuff quickly and year-round. There are a lot of incredible things that now exist and are going on in the world, Rok. Some of which I'm not sure you're ready to see or hear, or accept for that matter." The young man pauses before reentering his home, placing a hand on Rok's shoulder, a futile attempt to comfort him during this confusing time.

Back inside the sprawling mansion, they enter a different room from the one he woke in, one covered with wall-to-wall monitors.

"Look, I was checking this out earlier today just before you showed up. We had a serious storm. During the storm, nothing showed up on the screens. There's no helicopter on any of the cameras. Then, the moment the storm dissipates, the helicopter suddenly appears. Like out of nowhere, and on all the cameras."

Rok looks at the various television screens. Each of them displays images just as Pooky described. Rok scratches his head and Pooky nods his in confusion.

"I used to read about things like this. They're called myths or urban legends, or just fiction from c-books. I never knew if they were true or not, or what to really make of them. But I gotta ask, are you a time traveler?"

Rok tries to hide the weird smile on his face but can't. He laughs until he's in hysterics.

"Oh, please! How? What the heck are you talking about? I don't know. I'm just as confused as you are. I...what's with your watch and this house? What are c-books? Come on kid. Those damn grapes out there? White dudes can't run for president? Carnivore Trials? It's too much! You understand? It's just too much!"

Rok hears himself yelling the last few sentences and begins wondering if he might be on the brink of a nervous breakdown. He remembers what his mother would utter when she was having a particularly bad day.

"I'm going to have a nervous breakdown. I've worked hard for it. I deserve it and no one's going to deprive me of it!"

Suddenly, he runs from the room and makes his way outside the house. Once outside, he notices, for the first time, how eerily surreal the entire environment appears. *I gotta sit down,* he tells himself and does so on the porch steps below the front entrance to Pooky's house. Soon, a feeling of deep fatigue and bewilderment takes hold of Rok, and he finds himself with his head in hands, his body bent over and braced against the top of his legs. He feels a trembling vibration throughout his body. If he should figure out what's really happening here and what's troubling him, will it even matter if he accepts it or not? Won't any explanation guarantee madness?

At that moment, Pooky comes outside and takes a seat beside Rok.

"Come on, buddy, it's not all that bad. I mean, you do know where you're really from, right? Now you know what's going on, yeah? So... reality is real, you know. All we have to do is accept it."

"Kid, I don't know what's going on. I just remember listening to some funk while I was racing this dude from an intersection where we met. It seems like only a day or two ago," Rok pines, slumping further down in despair.

"Well let's go to the lab. Maybe we can find some answers and see what happened." Pooky consoles him. They make their way to the doorway of a room, which holds a vast array of advanced computer equipment and musical gear inside.

"Wow. What is all this stuff? Better yet, how'd you get it?" Rok glances around the room, taking it all in. It looks like some kind of control room meshed with a recording studio.

"Well, there's too much to explain in detail. But this here is the Wide World Web database," Pooky says while pointing toward the three-dimensional images appearing on a circular computer console situated on top of a two-inch thick and four-inch wide computer hard drive.

"A lot of this other stuff is for Pops and me. We're getting ready to make more music soon. We haven't worked on anything lately because we're suffering funk block. In 2083 one thing is constant: everything is hard to start, and creativity is really hard. It's damn near impossible to find inspiration these days."

"Then I guess finishing things has really got to be a bitch," Rok chides. "But what do you mean make *more* music?"

Rok suddenly feels a pang of excitement. If indeed he has somehow been transported seventy years into the future, then so be it. But at least they have music in the future, and composers. But what the hell happened to the rest of San Francisco? No matter. Rok finds solace knowing he is talking to someone who knows how to compose music. And this is enough to make him feel like a kid on Christmas morning or someone older who is about to play with the newest gadget on the market for adults.

"Here, I'll show you. Put this on." Pooky passes him an electronic device that appears to be some kind of headphone/helmet contraption.

Rok hesitates so Pooky places it on Rok's head then secures the slender chin-strap in place.

"Now think of a drum rhythm in your head. Whatever kind you want. The headgear will transpose your thoughts into percussion notation and the score will display on the computer in real time. Check it out."

Rok plays drums and a little bass guitar. Pooky has no way of knowing he's talking to a real musician, so he doesn't anticipate anything sophisticated coming from his time traveling friend. But Rok's "on the 1," and with ease thinks up a nifty drum rhythm. Literally through his thoughts, he creates an easy, structured drumbeat. Pooky excitedly shows him the notes being transposed onto a musical staff on the computer screen.

"Wow, you can see the measures, the whole musical

notation," Rok says, astounded by the technology. Rok then asks Pooky to erase what's been displayed on the computer screen so he can try another tune. This time Rok gets downright funky.

Watching the computer screen, Pooky can tell what Rok is creating in his head, and the sound it will make. In fact, he hits another key and instantly Rok's music starts to play throughout the lab. But Pooky almost instantly hits the escape key to erase what's been typed. His expression is one of panic.

"Dude, you can't do that!"

"Do what?"

"You're creating funk music and that's against the law! Da Man will find out. And when he does, he'll find us and finish us. We gotta set the safeguards."

"What? I can't do what? Create funk?"

"No funk...or pop or hip-hop or jazz or R&B or classical or anything good!"

"Give me a break and who is Da Man, dude?"

"Da Man is THE MAN! He controls all creativity. You'll seriously break the law if you try to do what you just did. I hope his network didn't catch on to us."

Pooky scrambles a bit, pressing buttons while looking up at the screen before it goes blank.

"I think we're okay."

"His network? What kind of communist world is this and what the hell is his network?"

"His network is the National Security System. It can detect anybody who creates or uses their imagination. Come on! You haven't heard of Da Man?"

"Hey, I've only been here a day or two, remember? Where I come from, everyone who's the man ain't crap! But wait, why is it wrong to be creative? Why can't an artist be an artist? Come on, kid, turn this thing back on and let me do it again," Rok demands.

Just then, the control room door is pushed all the way open and Pooky's father enters.

"Hey Pops, what's up?" asks Pooky, sounding somewhat nervous.

"Shit, who triggered the system?" his old man growls.

"Rok here did. He didn't know, and I wasn't prepared. His funk set it off."

"Yeah, that's true. I'm sorry. I didn't mean to set off any alarms," Rok wryly apologizes.

"So Rok's your name? I'm Billis, Pooky's dad. But look, we can't blow our cover. We must enable the proper safeguards before we ever get funky."

Rok gets up and walks over to shake Billis' hand.

There is a friendly greeting between them and the atmosphere in the room becomes more relaxed.

"By the way, how'd you get here?" Pooky's father suddenly asks. "It made a hell of a loud explosion, that old helicopter crashing in my vineyards. Where come from? How did all of you find such an ancient flying machine? I haven't seen one of those old contraptions since my first date with Pooky's mom at a museum. Why did you guys crash?"

"I'm not sure I can answer any of your questions, Sir," Rok replies.

"Rok came through the storm yesterday, that's what happened. It must have been a cosmic-electrical storm. It transported the helo and everyone on board through a wormhole. That's my theory for now," Pooky offers hastily.

"Can that be?" Billis asks skeptically. "The last cosmic-electrical storm on record was in 1985. I seem to remember something about a car…" His voice trails off.

"Well, from what I have concluded, this is 2083 and I'm seventy years in the future. I know I was living in 2010 and I'm pretty sure I was on that helicopter that crashed. But what the hell, I'm just a drag racer. What do I really know?" Rok sarcastically asks.

"Well, it's something we'll just have to figure out," Billis warmly answers. "Meanwhile, I'm curious about how you set off the house alarm. What kind of music was it that you were creating?"

"It was funk, Pops!" Pooky exclaims. "He was making funk!"

"He was?" Billis asks, an incredulous look on his face. "Listen to the drum beat he created."

As the music starts playing, a small line of worry creases the old man's brow. Still, he can't help but smile and feel a kinship with Rok.

"So, you're a creator?"

"I know how to play the drums and a little bass guitar when needed. But yeah, I've written a few tunes in my time."

"What? You know how to play musical instruments?" Billis almost screams, his voice full of excitement.

"I haven't heard of anyone playing an instrument of any kind anywhere in the world for over twenty years.

"Whoa! That's totally unacceptable. Now I wonder if I'm even on the right planet!" Rok quips.

"Well, Da Man and his powerful organization seek to destroy or control every musical instrument on earth, to make innovation even more impossible. As it is, there aren't many artists left in the world these days. One reason is because there are no instruments to play. Not openly anyway. Nothing musically can be accomplished on the Wide World Web. Musicians continue to disappear at an alarming rate. Billis' voice becomes strained, and a morose expression fills his countenance. This is not lost on Rok, who watches Pooky's slightly gray-haired dad defeatedly flop down into an Art-Deco sofa. The sofa is one of the few items of furniture in the white-washed room, which is otherwise bare except for the equipment and paraphernalia strewn throughout.

"The truth is, I've been trying to find musicians for years to help me make music. That's why I created this device you tried out. I invented it for me and Pooky so we could not only create, but do so undetected by the prying eyes and ears of Da Man. If he knew about my invention and our intentions, that'll be it for me...for us." He smiles wearily at his son.

"Da Man would have our heads and our musical hearts, too, if he could."

Rok and Pooky seat themselves in nearby computer chairs across from Billis to continue the conversation which becomes less encouraging to Rok by the second.

With an edge of stark emotion creeping into his voice, Billis continues, "I used to lead this popular group. It was called A Group Creating for All, but Da Man tried to finish me, permanently, as he did the majority of our band. Fortunately, his patrols have not been able to track me down though. They did find one of our camps five years ago and destroyed it. We have to be very careful. We have been labeled a terrorist organization and our surviving members are pursued all over the globe. We operate in small independent cells, sharing information and files when it is considered safe. That's why Pooky shut down the computer the moment you triggered the system with your funk. I need to set the program safeguards to accept creativity from you."

"Damn," Rok mutters. "This is some fanatical stuff. Like sci-fi or something from a comic book!"

"A c-book!" Pooky quickly says to him. "That's what a c-book is!"

"Well, your young son just keeps teaching me new things faster than I can unlearn the old!"

"Yes," Billis smiles, "my son can be didactic at times."

"Well, sir, I mean no disrespect. But I find myself in a pretty messed-up future. It's like a Nazi or communist state from what Pooky's told me. I'm accustomed to using my talents and abilities freely and doing what I want. But you say I can't create anything here in your time? You're saying it's against the law?"

"That it is," Billis reluctantly answers. "You see, Da Man wants total control of all people. He knew the entertainment industry had too much influence on people. So, he gradually organized a way to own it and control it, then he managed to regulate all creative thought and activity by artists everywhere. He has joined forces with most governments, making everyone subject to his rules and laws governing creativity...and doing anything original in life."

Rok shakes his head in disbelief. How did he arrive here in this totalitarian world, in this horrendous future? And why? More importantly, how can he escape? And how soon?

Billis notices the worry on Rok's face but presses on with his discourse to the young time traveler.

"The fact is simple: If any of Da Man's creativity rules or laws are broken—no matter how minor it may seem, like, say you use two words together to create a clever new phrase or fuse two unique notes of music, that person is immediately declared a criminal of the highest order, run through Judge Whitely's koala court, then given the same mind-breaking punishment as those before—exposure to Da Man's Ignoritis Machine.

"Koala court? The Ignoritis Machine?" Rok warily asks.

"It's koala now instead of kangaroo and yes," Billis explains, "it's a punishment far worse than the old punishment of mass bodily amputation. The Ignoritis Machine destroys more than one's body and limbs. It injects a lethal chemical that dissolves your intelligence and rational thought and blanks the sources of your imagination and ingenuity, resulting in Ignoritis, the latest man-made condition of misery."

"So mad scientists have been exceptionally busy in their labs since I was drag racing and sleeping in a coma!" Rok laughs.

"Well, you don't want any part of the Ignoritis Machine, this I guarantee you," Billis said. "It's insidiously brain-altering as well as brain-damaging!"

"I'll take your word for it. But I wonder, how can Da Man get away with all this nonsense? What about the government? The military?" Rok exclaims.

"He is the law!" both Billis and Pooky shout at the same time. Billis continues, "Da man has effectively rendered the government and law enforcement useless.

He controls everything."

"Well, okay then. So how can we get to him and stop this psycho crap? I mean, this ain't right. So, tell me, where can we find him? This big shot, Da Man?"

"Actually, my young new friend, I'm working on it," Billis confidently replies.

"Well, it don't make sense. Even the Soviets and North Korea didn't stop creativity. At least not like this! I don't understand how this can all be real," Rok laments.

Billis leans forward, the intensity in his eyes could bore a hole through Rok. "It's simple, Rok. When you own 90% of all entertainment entities, which equals power, you can do whatever you want."

"Truer words were never spoken!" chimes in Pooky.

"But none of these places you mention now exist, except for Co-Op China and a few Baltic states, France, Italy, and Germany. Less than half the United States is still populated or inhabitable. Wars and catastrophes have come and gone since your time, Rok. Much has happened to alter the face of the earth."

"So it seems," Rok sighs.

"However, we are working on an important project," Billis adds, "and we could use your help to take out Da Man and his organization and end his rule once and for all."

"Well, as long as I'm here and I have no other pressing matters, I'm game, I guess," Rok says. "Tell me more."

"I'm working on *The Funk Sonatra Project*. The goal is to sneak my way into the lives of all music fans, give them incredible eargasms, and then synchronize a method to purge the influence of Da Man from this un-artistic world for good. So, what I'm thinking is, and could use, is your creativity. I have a feeling that you have the fresh new sound I need."

"You mean the Frank Sinatra Project, right?" Rok asks.

"No. It's Funk Sonatra. With an O, not an I. Who's Frank?" Pooky asks back.

"Ol' Blue Eyes? Chairman of the Board? King of the Rat Pack? Francis Albert Sinatra. The Voice!"

"Well, we have no books or libraries, you know. Not for over fifty years now. Plus, almost every album and music cover of any kind have been abolished for decades. It's possible this Frank Sinatra you mention is who our Funk Sonatra is based on. Maybe one and the same. But did he really have blue eyes?"

Shaking his head, Rok smiles and coyly answers,

"Yep, Frank had blue eyes, and I guess in a way, he could be pretty funky when he wanted to."

"Exactly, like when we want to," says Pooky, smiling at both men. "The Funk Sonatra Project will be funky as well. Maybe as good as the music from this chairman singer you've mentioned. We likely just know him by a different name in our time, that's all. Maybe we have a little of his music still in decent condition and can do something interesting with it."

"No problem, I remember a lot of his tunes too," Rok states proudly.

"So, it's decided. Rok from 2010, you will help us?" Billis asks him in an almost pleading tone.

"If I can help you, I surely will," Rok replies, not entirely sure how.

"I want to create an album that will have all kinds of mellow, beautiful, soulful music. I'm hoping it will trigger people's innate love for music once again. Then it will generate natural creativity and people will be inspired again."

"I see," Rok slowly responds, although not actually seeing, but completely feeling the vibe.

"No lyrics, just music, mind you. Do you know this country hasn't seen a concert with a live band or orchestra in over four decades? I don't think you understand the full picture here. There are no more "out" musicians left on this earth. What's left of them are in hiding. I personally know of some still outside the U.S. hiding from the Da Man."

"Okay then, you can count me in," Rok tells Billis.

"Excellent!" Pooky's father replies. "With my technology, we will be able to create an album of music tracks in a short period of time. Outstanding tracks, I might add. We'll make it accessible to the people before Da Man can locate us through his electronic network. As long as he doesn't find us until after we put this out there, I'll be happy. I will have done my job." Standing up, he adds, "Young brother, I put my life on the line for art. For innovation. For creativity."

Like soldiers at attention, Rok and Pooky also come to their feet, and Rok again shakes Billis' hand. This time in a gesture of camaraderie, sealing their agreement and pledge.

"Then it's a deal. I now join you in The Funk Sonatra Project!" He turns his head to the side and says, "Ol' Blue Eyes, don't get mad just 'cause there won't be any singing!"

"So, we are unified!" chirps in Pooky.

"Yes, we are. Three heads are definitely better than two. Plus, with these tracks, we will help all who listen.

We will give them something to feel good about again when they listen to our music. We will give them creativity!"

"For sure," adds Pooky. Billis continues to direct his words to Rok.

"You know how music makes you feel certain ways, right? Well, we can change the way people feel and make them feel alive again. Hey, perhaps we can help establish world peace and justice. But first, we must stand up against Da Man, the half-man, half-computer creature who has ruined this country."

"Half-man, half-computer?" inquires Rok.

"Yeah, Rok," Pooky quickly answers. "He's a cyborg, man. A friggin' cyborg! Pretendin' to be human. But his heart's all nuts and bolts and microchips."

"Somehow, that doesn't surprise me. The way things have been going today, I don't put anything past anyone at this point," Rok says as he shakes his head incredulously.

"Well, no matter what he is," Billis adds. "This is what I'm willing to die for. The music these days, as it has been for years now, sounds like crap, and totally without any creativity. It is monotonous and lacking any depth. Computerized meaningless noise and repetition. I'm glad you have arrived my friend and are here now to help us make beautiful noise!"

"I did shake on it and I can dig where you're coming from. But hey, man, I'm still a little confused. How could our country and the world go in such a direction? Also, I want to be a part of this, I do, but I also want to return home to my own time, if I can."

"I understand," Billis nods.

CHAPTER EIGHT

THE PAST EXPLAINS THE FUTURE

ater that same day Rok, Pooky, and Billis resume their conversation while drinking grapeade and wine outside on the porch. Across the fields, the helicopter crash victims and most of the wreckage have been removed. A few hours earlier, Rok and Billis had taken some time out from their discussions to bury the bodies in well-dug, but unmarked, graves. At the least, they deserved a proper burial. Meanwhile, Pooky disposed of most of the debris via the disintegrating well in the back of the house. Now the three had some time to relax a little and discuss more in-depth a great many things, including The Funk Sonata Project.

"Well, this ongoing destruction of art does shock me like crazy," Rok begins. "I mean, you're basically saying that good music doesn't exist anymore? Creativity has become forbidden. So yeah, I want to help you create some music. Good music, that is. It's good too because you're in luck. Creating jams is something I love doing! But hey, man, you've got to promise to help me find a way back to my time when you can," Rok adds.

"No problem, my young friend," Billis answers. "First, let me tell you what else is going on in society today and the major things you've missed during your journey to our time period."

Billis leads his son and Rok back inside the house then over to a large computer console sitting on a wet bar in the living room. Still standing, he types at a feverish pace and within seconds, a huge wall screen displays all sorts of data and historical images. While this occurs, Billis begins relating the strange, violent, and dramatic history that entails over seventy years of change since Rok's memories of a former world and a very different time.

While Rok has been in a coma and until the time of his arrival at the vineyards, multiple significant events have occurred on earth. First, the ozone layer finally succumbed to extremely damaging levels and began exposing the planet to previously unknown forms of cosmic radiation. Though non-lethal to human beings, the cosmic rays killed 98% of all bird life on the planet. Chickens, once considered the main meat source in most parts of the world, were almost entirely wiped out. Because of this, many communities suffered a high deficiency in protein and other nutrients, and large numbers of the population fell ill and perished. Similarly, mad cow disease afflicted cattle and other farm animals worldwide, while fish and seafood across the globe became infected with a number of plagues. In effect, a large amount of these food sources ceased to exist and gradually led to the elimination of half the world's population. Throughout all this, the Carnivore Trials were held following the mass persecution of meat eaters who were accused of cruelty because of their diets. Farmers worked futilely to supply the population with enough fruit, vegetables, and grain but could not produce quickly enough.

In the meantime, numerous wars were waged and many nations were destroyed in all corners of the globe, resulting in them no longer existing. Large portions of the continents remain barren of people. In most places in the world, most people can barely afford sustenance of any kind. Soy, peanut products, and mass-produced perch farms have become the main sources of food for many.

Billis' history lesson is a horrifying one, and Rok longs to return to the past and would even prefer his unconscious state rather than live in the reality of what has befallen the human race. What a terrible future awaits all those in Rok's past. He wonders what Ol' Blue Eyes would think and have to say.

Rok notices Billis has more to read from the mounted plasma screen, and he braces himself to be subjected to more ghastly data and images to make his education complete. Much more.

"Scientists determined the earth would be able to sustain human life for roughly fifty years. The United World Government began traveling to Mars. At first, our leaders were searching for oil and other sources of energy. Then after a few years, people from every part of the world sent spacecraft filled with a new breed of pioneers and volunteers to colonize the red planet. But all this exploration ultimately amounted to nothing."

"Around that same time, young males from the poorer sectors of society were imprisoned and had their DNA extracted with the goal of creating a clone work force to serve as slaves to those selected "superior individuals" who began building a new race of humankind on this "new home world" of Mars."

Billis grows silent, and the three of them read on,

each to himself, as the powerful graphic images following this chronicle feel like knives stabbing them and numbing all of their frail senses. Rok begins to wonder if there was any contribution he could make to repair the tragic state of humankind. Can music make a difference? Was there any kind of creativity any man or woman could cogitate to undo the events and sad state of affairs humankind had miserably undergone and achieved?

While Rok is thinking these troubling thoughts, Billis exhaustively sits down and tells them to read the rest of the history lesson on their own. Pooky turns away, and Rok stands, mesmerized by the continuing history lesson both son and father have suffered and were now imploring to him.

And so, it went on. After decades of military resources being stretched thin all across the globe, and with its own nonstop war on terror, the United States became unable to even police its own borders and the rebellion brewing. What ensued was a period in which those in power (called the Saintimorians) began "the cleansing," which consisted of exterminating all distinct races and ethnic groups in the Tri-Continental United States. The goal was to create one homogenous society so that no individual would have ties or loyalties to any particular ethnic group. Thus, the Procreation Act was declared. By 2030, what existed was one North American nation that included the United States, Canada, Mexico, and most of Central America.

Using the Super Highway as a conduit, hate groups from all over the hemisphere were contracted out as mercenaries and hired to conduct elimination attacks on creative, free-thinking, freedom-loving people nationwide who were of course, the new minorities. The attacks still take place as they did the first time they occurred—midnight on December 24, 2020. Yearly, an estimated 50,000 freedom-loving minorities lose their lives, or even worse, they are subjected to the Ignoritis Machine.

Suddenly, Rok shouts, "Wait! What? Get the hell out of here. It isn't that bad is it? Come on. I can't believe it. You mean minorities have no power or wealth to fight back?" Rok asks angrily.

"There are no more minorities, not as you know them, anyway. The increased sense of community and cultural identity threatened the New World Order, leading to the Procreation Act. The power they began to yield dissipated as assimilation spread. For example, Black Americans earned tons of money in the entertainment and sports industries years ago, and when they started recycling dollars back into their own communities, there was a strong push by anti-ethnicity forces. Just as they started divesting in gaudy jewelry, diamonds and material things, the price values dropped, depriving the government of needed funds. The government couldn't have that happen. The financial depression that followed made it easy for Da Man to introduce alternatives to the government, and here we are."

"But surely it wasn't just white people who created this situation and did all this?" pleads Rok.

"No," Billis answers. "It was inheritors and the un-earning rich, politicians, and greedy people of every race. However, this was one of the main reasons minorities lost the opportunity for wealth and power. As they grew stronger, the Establishment grew weaker. No longer able to control them with money wasted on worthless investments with no return, they pretty much banned being Black or Latino, or even white for that matter, and demanded the mixing of the races until no traces of ethnicity existed."

"I see," said Rok, although not *totally* seeing what Billis was saying.

"Descendants of the American slave trade tried to fight for reparations, you know," Pooky's father continued. "The '40 Acres and a Mule' form of reparations. But that got shut down many times. They weren't treated like other races that entered the country and were able to get some form of reparations. The reasons for it not being provided remain secret and under lock and key, just like the cure for AIDS, which is a disease that was planted in Africa. There is still no answer on how they kept this information from the public. Have you heard of AIDS?"

"Oh, yeah," Rok sadly replies.

"But like this?" Pooky suddenly asks. "AIDS...Africa is dying, shit."

"I hear ya, son. Africa *was* dying. But watch your language!"

"No problem. I know what it really stands for. Acquired Immune Deficiency Syndrome. It's a sexually transmitted disease, supposedly. You die from it. Some say it's a man-made disease designed to eliminate communities. But what do you mean, Africa *was* dying?"

"Well, I'm glad to see that there is some history you already know and do not need to be taught. To answer your question, Africans got smart and learned from their own history. Once they saw what was happening in the west, Africa became stronger and a federation to protect the interests of all African nations was formed. Collectively, they decided to close its borders and protect its people and resources. Now referred to as the Bright Continent, Africa remains the only land in the world where AIDS has been eradicated, innovation and creativity are openly encouraged, and people live free from tyranny." Billis states with admiration in his voice.

Images stop filling the screen, so Pooky hits a few keys on the computer's keyboard and the screen turns black. For a moment, Pooky and his father stare at Rok, uncertain of what to say next.

"Well then," Rok begins, while getting to his feet and smiling humbly at both of them. "I'm glad to be brought up to date. I mean, I'm stuck here in your time period, so I might as well know the whole layout of things. Knowing the whole history up to now only makes me want to help you more."

Billis stands up and returns Rok's smile. "I'm glad, we can certainly use your help."

"I definitely have plenty of reasons to help you and do my part to bring justice and equal rights back to society and all people, and to help people enjoy freedom together. I do believe music can achieve this. Music can certainly express it in powerful ways.

Prophets like Bob Marley, Fela Kuti, Bob Dylan, Jackson Browne, George Clinton, and even Ol' Blue Eyes, to name just a few, were able to open people's minds and spread the truth. 'Free your mind and your ass will follow,' were the great words of Sir Clinton."

"They still ring true my friend," Billis tells him while patting him on the back. "His words live in you, and now will live in all three of us. For years, books, music, and creativity have gradually been subverted and smothered and even destroyed. But it ain't hardly enough to stop The Funk Sonatra Project!"

"Not hardly!" Pooky enthusiastically adds.

"Well, I don't know how to save a race of people, nor am I trying to do that. I just want people to have a chance to feel good again instead of always being angry and desperate and miserable and feeling jealous of one another. I'd like to inspire them to reach for the sky with their own aspirations and dreams while helping others. And get the courage to stand up against Da Man, Co-Op China, and other tyrants to reclaim their freedom."

Thinking about everything they've been through and the possibilities contained within this moment, Billis breathes a sign of relief, a sense of empowerment washing over him.

CHAPTER NINE

LET THERE BE MUSIC

After a delicious dinner of tiny perch and frog parts from Billis' backyard pond, as well as a host of peanut-derived dishes, the three artists adjourn to their respective bedrooms in Billis' home and fall asleep quickly to enjoy a good night's rest.

Early the next afternoon, the energy in the house is electric as animated conversation reverberates throughout.

"Oh yeah, that's the one," says Rok, excitedly. "Rewind it and listen to the drums on that track. That's crossed up with the flute and that crazy bass line. That's funky! Man, that's like the twentieth song we've made today. This gadget your dad invented is the hippest thing. We've got all kinds of music from it. This is how you make music, man! It brings everything together so fast!"

"Yes it is," Pooky says while smiling at Rok.

"So, you know that if the public gets their hands on this, people might feel free again to listen to music? They won't be programmed to only listen to music Da Man broadcasts."

"You mean *when* they get their hands on it!" corrects Pooky.

"Yeah, you right. Play song number nine. Yeah, that's the one."

"That's really why my dad calls this The Funk Sonatra Project. He envisions this collection of music wrapped up in one neat package to appeal to a huge audience," Pooky chuckles.

"Well, he's given us a lot to work with and create from. Between the three of us, we're one helluva band and I'm sure we've got ourselves the next album of the year. Hell, the millennium!"

The three of them have been at it all day, working feverishly in Billis' music/control room, laying down tracks and creating songs for what will become The Funk Sonatra Project.

Rok and his docile friend decide to take a break and ransack the kitchen for a midday snack. Rok secretly hopes there is something good to eat. Pooky and Billis have been extremely kind and welcoming, but one can only eat so many peanuts.

Soon, the two young men sit devouring peanut butter and grape jam sandwiches washed down with tall glasses of almond milk. Billis returns from a long nap and joins them. He wastes no time informing them that he plans to put The Funk Sonatra Project on the map immediately. There are still plenty of underground television and radio stations and nightclubs all over the world to which he has access. Plus, there are still many independent power brokers in the music and entertainment industry not under Da Man's thumb who he knows he can interest in the project. Finally, he has found a way to hack into Da Man's network. From there he can broadcast the tunes. It's risky because he will be exposed. That will be the point of no return, so Billis knows it has to be worth it.

As it is, Pooky is always present when his father is involved in negotiations and Billis has taught him the business side of music production well. Since Rok has his own experience with the creation and production of music, the three of them are more than ready to set The Funk Sonatra Project into motion.

Thus, Billis and Pooky immediately set up a meeting with a large entertainment entity in Germany to be held that night. This rather large company handles a wealth of musical enterprises, especially when it comes to international promotion and distribution, and that's what Billis needs for his project. The good thing is, Da Man and his partner in crime, the Sociocractic Co-Op of China, are not so powerful in Europe or in certain parts of Asia. If *The Funk Sonatra Project* can achieve success in these regions, there is a good chance it can also get a foothold in the United States.

After making arrangements for an overnight stay in Germany, Billis and Pooky leave in haste to meet with the underground entertainment conglomerate. They do so via private jet from a nearby, hidden airfield, both of which Billis owns. Rok is left to keep watch over the estate and vineyards during their time away. He sees the time as an opportunity to thoroughly search the whole property for food of any kind that has absolutely nothing to do with peanuts or tiny little fish!

CHAPTER TEN

LET THERE BE LOVE

Reclining comfortably in a Hippie beanbag in Billis' control/music lab, Rok enjoys himself while listening to the songs he and his two fellow artist friends created. At the same time, he's reading the latest news from the console of a floating rectangle laptop. The device, he decides, is almost as cool as the music of Ol' Blues Eyes himself. A mixture of positive and negative emotions consume him. While he really enjoys the music the three of them created, the conditions under which they were created cause him angst.

He is all at once saddened and enraged about the events that have occurred over the last seventy years. A balanced mix of disgust and anger creep in whenever Da Man's name is mentioned.

"The Man of Metal & Savage Heart," as some

independent media outlets are able to get away with calling him, reminds Rok of Mafia godfathers who wrought terror during the 20th century, and the rich, fat-cat CEOs who attempted to take over the American economy and rule the world and ghetto-rife financial districts from skyrise office buildings. However, all the music, reading, and deep thinking have sent Rok into sensory overload. He is famished, he realizes, and knows the growling in his stomach refuses to be ignored any longer.

Fortune had been on his side earlier that afternoon. He had discovered Billis' hidden cache: a refrigerator and three deep freezers containing tons of satiating normal food Billis keeps locked away in a secret pantry near the kitchen. That's where he now heads. A well-stocked, state-of-the-art storage facility filled with a cornucopia of mouth-watering delicacies has made living in this horribly afflicted future almost palatable to Rok. However, the prospect of having to live out the rest of his life in this era is not something he is yet ready to contemplate. After all, one must eat and obtain sustenance before he can be expected to deal with such complex subjects as the past, present, and future!

Upon opening the refrigerator door, he can't believe his eyes. There, staring him in the face, is a huge meaty-looking casserole, and just beyond that sits what is the biggest German chocolate cake he's ever laid his ravenous eyes upon. *Which should I devour first?* He considers to himself. *Cake or casserole?*

At that moment, while bending over, reaching for a jar of mustard from inside the fridge, he hears an unmistakable sound: the click of a trigger being cocked on a gun from behind him.

His head half inside the appliance, he hits the back of it on the freezer door while trying to turn around and face the unknown assailant behind him. However, this is not what causes him to drop the jar of mustard which shatters on impact. Not hardly, he muses. For a moment he forgets about the gun and is captivated by the angelic apparition standing but a few feet away from him. It is a darkly dressed woman of inconceivable beauty who, for some reason, seems as startled by his looks and appearance as he is by hers.

Still, the intrusion catches him completely off guard. He has a keen sense of hearing and an acute sixth sense. So how did she sneak up on him like this? He notices she's wearing thick-heeled boots. So now he has reason to feel more than moderately ashamed. How did he not hear her? Regardless, what's to fear? *Yeah, there's a huge revolver in her hand pointed directly at me. But she is oh so fine!*

Hmm, she teases herself. *Who is this fine specimen of masculinity? Back to the business at hand*, she admonishes herself. *No time for flustering!*

"Okay, forget the mustard. Where are they?" she asks Rok. She is, Agent Nzinga 5000 from Wu-Killers, Inc. She is on a very important mission that must be met with no delays or distractions. No matter how cute and attractive the distraction! "Hey, I am not into playing games or asking questions twice!"

Stepping to the side and closing the fridge door, Rok is still mesmerized by Nzinga's exquisite beauty and the black, form-fitting leather tights she's wearing. *Wow! What a knock-out! Oh, wow, what a huge gun.*

"Answer me!" she gestures with the pistol.

"Hey, do you honestly think I'm *not* going to obey you with you pointing that...that cannon at me? Not cool, lady!"

Rok smiles and shakes his head, but keeps his eyes fixed on the large, long-barreled weapon aimed at his torso. "Damn, what kind of gun is that anyway? Any relation to a bazooka?" At this, he notices that a slight smile actually creases her lips.

"So, tell me, what is it that you want?" Rok calmly asks.

Raising one well-arched eyebrow, and in an equally

calm voice, she replies, "Anything I want, mister, I can have. I can fight armored vehicles with this." For emphasis, she points the gun closer to Rok's head.

"Shhhhh, chill with the hard ass vernacular, lady. As sexy as you are, I know you've stopped more than tanks in their tracks. More like all the tank drivers the world has ever known."

Nothing like kind words and compliments, Rok speculates, *to get on this kickass-looking dame's good side. Yeah, that's what she is. A dame. A sexy one at that! Exactly what Frank would call her.*

"You shhhhh! I'm asking the questions here. Where's Billis and the kid?"

"They just left for Germany on business, that's where. Why don't you tell me what you need and maybe I can help? Cause I'm starving here and I'd like to get back to fixing myself some food. You can watch my every move. I'm not in any hurry to get shot by that huge crater-maker of yours!"

Lowering his arms to his side and leaning on the counter behind him, Rok tries his best to look as unthreatening as possible.

"Come on, lady, what's up? Who are you?"

Noticing her thin smile turning to a frown, he makes his voice even more servile. "You know what, you don't even have to answer that, or any of my questions for that matter. However, I do wish to comment at this time, if you don't mind, that you are no doubt, *the* finest woman I have..."

"Oh, shut up!" she interrupts in a flustered tone. "What's your name?"

"I'm Rok. Just Rok."

"Rok, huh," Nzinga 5000 says, seemingly suspicious. But what she's really feeling is an unusual sensation, and not one she's ever had to deal with while on a mission. Strangely, the sensation is both pleasant and disturbing at the same time. She feels warm all over, with a tingling stir moving across the nape of her neck and back. She finds it almost unnerving, these strange emotions intensifying inside her. *What the hell! Such emotions must not occur during an assignment!* She's trained to keep her emotions in check. All emotions, in fact. For when she kills, she feels neither satisfaction nor remorse. She is trained to be impersonal and cold.

"Take your clothes off and strip down," she orders Rok.

"Gosh, lady, we only just met!" Rok smirks. Seeing his humor having no effect upon her, he begins removing his clothing as ordered. As he does so, item by item, Nzinga 5000 finds herself becoming turned on. Rok is not only naturally handsome, but his body is muscular and well-defined. His smooth, dark skin a contrast to the white-washed surroundings. His speech, so cool and confident. Everything about him arouses her. Is it possible any man could arouse her both sexually and mentally at the same time? At first sight?

Having placed his clothes in a neat pile on the kitchen floor between them, Rok is now down to his blue boxer shorts and hoping something might intervene to save him from complete immodesty.

"What's that music playing?" She suddenly asks. "Where's it coming from?"

Damn! The Funk Sonatra Project. I forgot to turn it off! He hollers inside his head. *She's here because of it. Da Man must have sent her. To destroy the music and us!*

"Look, if you're here for the music, I'll take you to it."

"Show me," she replies, and immediately uses the gun to position him so she can tie his hands behind his back, while enjoying the view of Rok from behind. She's ashamed of this but is unable to pry her eyes off of him...and the view of his cute backside!

"Move," she shoves him in the lower back with the gun. "Take me to the music."

As they head for Billis' lab, they brush against each

other once or twice, each time both of them feeling an intoxicating warmth and attraction for the other. Just from this slight physical contact, she finds her body becoming increasingly warm in certain places. The gun feels slippery in her sweaty palm.

At the same time, Rok is trying to walk in such a manner to keep his own libido under wraps. *Literally*, he jokes to himself. *So far, so good*, he glares. *No lengthy protrusions reaching out in front!*

Finally, both of them exhale, the lab at last. Inside the control/music room, The Funk Sonatra Project is playing and is loud and clear. Its swinging rhythm immediately serves to create a sense of additional harmony between the two of them.

"It's a very pleasant sound," Nzinga whispers, uncertain if she had spoken such forbidden words. Placing her gun inside the holster under her left arm, she quickly removes a sharp knife and cuts the rope binding Rok's hands behind his back. For a tender moment, they stop and gaze into each other's eyes. The music continues to weave a calming effect over the female assassin, and Rok finds himself wondering where this stunning beauty has been all his life.

"Here, listen to this," Rok quietly suggests, and without resisting, she lets him approach the stereo computer and punch a key that changes the music to another track. He switches to a mellow, seductive jazz-like track. Nzinga is mesmerized by the slower music, just as he hoped she would be.

However, Rok's first thoughts are to pacify her, and thus save himself from injury or death. He is satisfied that his life is no longer in danger. Now the task at hand is to achieve supreme intimacy with this lovely female and get her to remove as much clothing as he has.

Nzinga finds herself totally absorbed, almost hypnotized by the sultry music. She drops the sharp blade in her hand, and with a dull thud it impales itself, sticking upright from the hardwood floor.

Rok turns, places his hands over her bare arms, and asks, "You like what you hear? Yes?"

"Yes."

"How about what you see?" Rok gently whispers.

She feels breathless and knows at this point that the act of seduction is taking place. *Where have I put my gun? And the knife which I have used so efficiently so many times in the past, where in the world did I leave it? Hmm. How did his hands get untied? But they feel so good caressing my arms and shoulders.* Her thoughts cause her shock and shame. *I should have shot him before he dropped that jar of mustard! But he looked so cute*, she bemoans to herself. She notices now that he looks even cuter, coyly smiling at her while struggling to get her tight ninja suit unzipped and stripped off of her.

Rok suddenly feels certain that the year 2083 is the year of his destiny. Frank and his Rat Pack pals somehow planned this whole scenario. Doesn't matter how. They just did. Every single one of them was a hunk and a cool dude. Rok was meant to save the future and here is his reward: the most awesome kickass chick ever to wield a gun! The future was meant for him, and he was here to save it. That's what he can hear Frank telling him. For Frank, "The Chairman of the Board," Sinatra was never one to mince words. Not in any song he sang. Not in any film he made. And not in the life he lived. Just ask Dino or Sammy or Joey or Peter. The Rat Pack. They'll tell you. They told Rok.

The two about-to-be-lovers stand caught in the moment. His eyes roam over her sensuous, gorgeous body, then stare into her soft, brilliant eyes. Just then, both seem to speak an unspoken language of desire. She moves even closer to him and reaches up to untwist and release the large coils of silky, ebony hair covering her head. It falls in wavy cascades down her bare bronze back, almost reaching the top of her shapely buttocks and curvaceous hips.

Rok has never seen or ever touched such a dazzling creature. He tells her that. He tells her God must have spent a ton of extra time creating her. They both find themselves completely naked, swaying to the funky sound of "Come Fly With Me," a unique musical interpretation that Rok is more than proud to have helped create. It's as if this too, was destined.

The whole experience is new for Nzinga 5000. She felt sensual, sexual, and amorous attraction for a target, even though technically, Rok is not a direct target. But just the same, he dwells in the lair of targets and her enemy. *What the hell*, she sighs. The music is intoxicating and so liberating. *I'm tired of death and mayhem and violence and killing. Love and lust are so much more fulfilling!* A strange thought lodges itself in her brain, one she remembers hearing once as a child. *"Make love, not war!"* Yes, her thoughts whisper in Rok's ear and form words she's never spoken previously. "Let's make love."

"You took the words right out of my mouth, babe," Rok responds. Without wasting a second, he stretches out an arm, finds the computer stereo remote, turns up the volume and hits the "repeat track" key as many times as his wandering, free hand possibly can.

CHAPTER ELEVEN

REGROUPING THE MIX

The next day arrives with luxuriant sunshine and a warm breeze, and Rok awakes with a smile in his heart and a big grin on his face. But it is short-lived, for he quickly notices he is alone. Nzinga has gone. He grabs the cellphone watch Pooky left him and dials the number Billis provided in case he needed to reach them while they were away. With no time for small talk, Rok hastily informs Billis about the previous evening's events, leaving out a few details concerning Da Man's lovely assassin, the one Da Man sent to kill them.

Within an hour, Billis and his son are on his private jet and flying back to the vineyards.

Billis' double-supersonic aircraft arrives in less than two hours, and he wastes no time checking the estate's cameras to ascertain how Nzinga 5000 got past his sophisticated security network.

Rok believes Nzinga shares the same feelings he does for her and that she can become an ally to The Funk Sonatra Project. Maybe they can persuade her to leave her current employers and instead join their cause, and even take out Da Man himself. Obviously, if she can get by Billis' complicated security system undetected, she has a shot at taking on Da Man's organization and getting to him.

One of the estate's surveillance cameras managed to capture a clear image of Nzinga 5000.

With this photo in hand, Billis spends a few hours researching online and learns that Nzinga 5000 is a hired hit woman working for Wu-Killers, Inc. in Co-Op China. Co-Op China is Da Man's number one supplier of weapons, drugs, and manpower in his struggle to achieve greater rule over North America. Da Man has never sent an assassin after him before. He must know about The Funk Sonatra Project and not just the fact that Billis and his freedom fighters are still alive and working to overthrow his regime. As if they did not already feel pressure to move quickly and cautiously, a renewed sense of urgency washed over them regarding the entire situation. Billis knows now that The Funk Sonatra Project must be disseminated as widely as possible immediately, particularly in California and New York, where Da Man wields a lot of power.

Fortunately for everyone concerned, Billis has agents and contacts of his own to help with the cause. Soon they are updated with more news. A double agent informs them of the following: after Nzinga left the estate, she contacted her controllers at Wu-Killers, Inc. to tell them she wanted out of the organization and begged to be released to start a new life for herself. In response, Wu-Killers dispatched one hundred of their top agents to find and capture her. Sadly, they were successful. Since she failed to carry out her orders and complete her mission, and because her insubordination is so extreme and her loyalty cannot be guaranteed, Wu-Killers plans to subject her to the machine to wipe her mind clean so they can educate and train her all over again.

Billis is not just a good guy. He's a good guy with means. In fact, his wealth rivals that of Da Man himself, although he is able to claim he came by it through honorable and honest hard work. Before going underground, Billis had been a giant in Silicon Valley. He was a silent partner with some of the largest tech firms before the bubble burst, often appearing in lists of the wealthiest this and that. Billis liquidated his cash to fund the resistance prior to going off the grid. At this point, Nzinga needs the resistance as much as it needs Nzinga.

After brokering a deal with the help of Swiss agents, Billis agreed to pay a twenty-five million dollar dowry, if you will, securing the release of Nzinga 5000 from Wu-Killers. A huge price to pay, the three of them agree, but with Nzinga 5000 on their side, they just might have a chance of getting The Funk Sonatra Project released and destroying Da Man's evil organization.

After wiring the money and with a written agreement in hand, we find Billis sitting impatiently on a bench outside the Wu- Killers, Inc.'s San Francisco facility. Strolling nearby, and with equal impatience, are Pooky, and their new friend and fellow musician, Rok. It's been two hours of silent waiting. No one is feeling it worse than Rok, who is eager to hold Nzinga in his arms once again. But will Wu-Killers, Inc. hold up their end of the bargain? Will they release her? Will he ever kiss her soft, sensual, full lips again? At that moment, as worrisome thoughts filter through his mind, Rok notices a sudden motion from the side of the building. Not from the front entrance, but from a side door some thirty yards away, Rok and his two friends watch three individuals exit the building. Rok doesn't need to strain his eyes to recognize the woman in front of her two armed escorts. It's definitely Nzinga 5000!

He cannot suppress the smile he feels in his heart, which has become a wide grin on his face. However, just as he is about to hurry toward her, Nzinga turns and delivers a sweeping leg kick to the two guards strolling behind her. Her karate blow is swift and lethal, as both men are knocked off their feet and unconscious.

"Just so you'll never forget me," she yells, looking down at the two flattened men with utter disdain.

Rok rushes to welcome her into his embrace as she turns away from the two fallen men.

"Gosh babe," why did you do that?"

"Oh, I don't know. Just because, I guess," she smiles coyly, then kisses him passionately on the lips.

"Well, I hope they have health insurance in this era! They'll need it," Rok chuckles.

They share a long kiss and embrace, until finally, she steps back to gaze into his searching eyes.

"I couldn't do it, you understand. I was hired to kill Billis and anyone else in his house. But I couldn't. I can't be a hired assassin anymore. You did something to me that I don't understand. Something I've never felt before. But something I want to feel forever. You know?"

"Yes baby, I know," he smiles.

"It was unforgettable and so much more fun than killing!"

"Well, it was unforgettable for me too," Rok says answering her with another quick kiss. "Being apart from you just these few hours has been killing me! But come on, we're together now and will always be. No matter what, and we've got a lot of life to live," he pauses as he watches Billis and Pooky approach. "We also have some very important work to do"

Billis and Pooky are amazed at Nzinga's beauty and notice how well matched she is to Rok's rugged, cool looks. If they didn't understand before, it is clear to them now, his desperation to get her back. His voice is ebullient when he introduces her to them.

"Hey guys, this is Nzinga..." Rok begins.

"No, no longer is it that. My real name is Anna LaRue. Please call me Anna," she quickly interrupts.

Rok is intrigued by this revelation. But not missing a beat, he says, "Well then, this is Anna, and Anna, this is Billis and his son Pooky."

They exchange friendly greetings and short hugs.

Then Billis steps forward to interrupt the festivities and remind Rok that they need to get moving, dire tasks await them.

With Billis and Pooky in the lead, Rok and Anna continue hugging and kissing while following a few paces behind. Meanwhile, Pooky keeps rubbing his eyes, hoping in vain to remove the glazed expression on his face.

"How am I ever going to get a chick like her?" Pooky whines.

"Shush son! She probably has elevated hearing or something with all her other...eh, superior attributes. You don't ever want to piss her off, that's for sure. Not with the way she can kick!"

They reach Billis' vehicle, a fancy, refurbished retrofitted 1968 Mustang. Rok holds out his hand and Billis drops the key into it. Rok immediately hops in behind the wheel, with Anna taking the passenger seat beside him.

"Let me show you how a car like this should be driven," challenges Rok. Without further ado, he puts the pedal to the metal, and the four of them speed away from Wu-Killers, Inc. at drag racing speed!

CHAPTER TWELVE

A QUICK EXCHANGE

Deep under the White House, inside Da Man's underground sanctuary, we hear a faint, quivering voice announce, "Master, we have a serious problem."

"I'm getting fairly tired of your *serious problems* and nothing but negative reports all the time," bellows Da Man.

"Well, it's not my fault, master. I'm just the messenger!"

"Really? Ya think? So, what it is this time, messenger of bad news!"

"Well, eh...it seems that the contract on Billis and the others was not carried out. It appears the Wu-Killers agent reneged on the assignment and...well, this is unusual...unheard of."

"What?" Da Man asks, getting up from the plush

sofa and directing his gaze at the computer screen over Whitely's shoulder.

"She's been discharged from their service. Someone bought her ownership and we have word that Billis and his aids created something new. Something really powerful that might damage our plans. It's more of that great, I mean, terrible and problematic, music we recently heard."

"You mean The Funk Sonatra Project, right? What a stupid name!" Da Man snaps.

"Yes sir, it is that," Whitely obediently agrees.

"So why are you telling me all this?" Whitely's master loudly asks.

"I thought I told you not to come back and not to bother me until Billis was taken out and the job was done. With such a pea-size brain, how did you ever become a judge or an attorney for that matter!"

"Well, you appointed me, sir, and..."

"Oh, shut up! Your incompetence is insufferable! Verily you shall suffer dire consequences for this newest foul-up. But first, alert our national security units here in the region, and anywhere else our little band of patriots may have gone off to. Let everyone know that there is a contract on his head. Ten million to whoever brings me his head, and I mean just that. I want his severed head brought to me!

Shuddering before his master's clamorous voice, Whitely begins typing twice as fast to implement Da Man's orders.

"And there's a million on his imbecile son's head and another million on the head of that drag-racing clown who's traveled here from the past. Whatever his idiot name is.

"Stone, I think," utters Whitely.

"No, that's not it, you dummy. Hmm. Boulder perhaps. Or pebble. No, something to do with music."

"Roll," Whitely perilously ventures.

"No, not Roll, you moron! Rok! It's Rok. That's his name! Make it five million for his head, too."

"Yes, master," whimpers Whitely, with a tinge of relief in his voice.

CHAPTER THIRTEEN

THE PLOT THICKENS

At the estate, Billis' computer is busy retrieving information from the underground wire services regarding the worldwide contract that's been put out on him, Pooky, and Rok. The contract also includes a woman fitting Anna's description.

"Well," Billis sneers, "the mechanical man has been busy today, hasn't he? Fortunately, so have I, bug scum! So have I."

***

A short time later, and with the others present inside his lab, Billis' computer suddenly coughs out a special alert sheet. Earlier, Billis had programmed a request. The sheet contains the address and location of Da Man's secret underground residence.

The four of them let out a cheer to celebrate

receiving this vital information, but Billis' stern countenance calms them down. He knows he must not only get The Funk Sonatra Project distributed in key places and heard by as many people as possible, but they also must take out Da Man and destroy his organization's leadership if they are to save the world and restore freedom and innovation to the people. All four of them are painfully aware of this.

"Now we have Da Man's location. Even most of his travel routine. Nothing can stop us!" He pauses to read the computer printout. Then, in a little less positive tone, continues. "Whoa, get this. His pad is right under the White House in WDC. It's thirty floors directly below the Oval Courtroom."

"Wow," sighs Pooky.

"How could he get such a hideout built? Right under everyone's nose? Don't you have any police or government agencies of any kind to protect from such a thing? I just don't get it." Rok wonders.

"I told you before, the government is at best powerless and complacent when it comes to Da Man. Some authorities may even be on his payroll. His sanctuary may have been built centuries ago, who knows? He holed up there after he acquired power over most of the government and authorities throughout

WDC and elsewhere. The *how* is not important. It's the *what* that is, and what we're going to do in order to free creativity," Billis responds. "I have a plan."

"While Pooky and I return to Germany to finish this international deal and get The Funk Sonatra Project started, you and Anna can infiltrate the White House to get to Da Man."

"How are we going to get through to his hideout and through all the security?" Rok asks, a worried look on his face.

Billis points at Anna.

"With her special talents and skills, that's how. Remember?"

Anna nods her head and smiles confidently at them.

"Ha! It'll be a piece of cake. One of my assignments took place inside the White House and I know many ways to get in. But first, I'll need to gather some specialized equipment from my safe house here in the city if we're going to make this all happen."

Smiling in a deliciously wicked manner, she saunters over and flops down onto Rok's lap and lays her head against his chest. Feeling a little embarrassed, Rok smiles at Billis, but has no idea what to say.

"You two lovebirds don't get too comfortable. We

have lots to do," Billis grins. "For now, me and Pooky are back off to the Rhineland to get the deal sealed for The Funk Sonatra Project. I'll be in touch. You two, be careful!"

Later, with Billis piloting, he and Pooky buckle up inside his private jet. They take off and travel at double supersonic time on their way to Germany. Elsewhere, Rok and Anna board an underground Bullet train to WDC. During the two-hour trip, they manage to find a private cabin and sufficient time for some serious intimacy of the most up-close-and-personal kind!

CHAPTER FOURTEEN

TRAVEL TIME

Later, just before their train arrives in WDC, Anna tells Rok about a distinctive device Wu-Killers surgically implanted inside her chest cavity when she was a child, before becoming a full-fledged assassin. It is a small explosive attached to her heart and wired to explode should her heart ever stop beating or the device somehow became disconnected from her heart. Essentially, she was programmed to self-destruct.

Rok is quite distressed upon hearing this information, and Anna endeavors to console him. At least the device cannot be detonated by any other means, and there is infinitesimally little chance the wiring could malfunction or become disconnected in any manner. She tells Rok that she too believes in the cause of creativity and people being free to create as they wish.

The fact is, since a young child, her secret passion had always been to be an artist, a singer. Maybe even an opera singer rather than a trained assassin driven only to kill. She knows her dream of artistic creativity is probably at an end. Her mind no longer even allows such thoughts. This is why she feels that the mission with Rok, Billis, and Pooky is so important. She is willing to give up her life, if need be, to see it achieve success.

Rok implores her to stay behind and let him carry on the mission without her. But she reminds him that only she can get both of them into the White House and Da Man's underground hideout, and only she is physically capable of defeating Da Man in armed combat, and successfully handling the violent threat that awaits them.

With a tear in his eye, he reluctantly concedes to her arguments and takes her into his arms. Only seconds, that seem like a lifetime, lapse for the brave duo to comfort each other, then the super-fast train pulls into the WDC station.

Their passage through the WDC train terminal is brief, and Rok, with credentials provided to him by Billis, is able to rent an inconspicuous white cargo van. A half hour later, they find themselves parked a short block away from the Presidential Palace. It is almost nightfall now, and extended shadows continue their creeping advance over the bustling city.

Inside the back of the van, Rok and Anna work in silence, preparing for the most daunting part of the mission, getting inside the White House safely and without being observed. Both have attired themselves in black face paint and the stealth uniform of the ninja. They are also heavily armed and prepared for anything.

Further darkness envelops WDC, and zero hour is almost at hand. Anna opens the large briefcase she acquired from her safe house in San Franco and begins removing items. Some objects are foreign to Rok, and Anna quickly explains each gadget's function and operation.

Finally, she uses a high-end, high-speed laptop to designate and pinpoint the location of Da Man within a foot of accuracy. He is less than a quarter of a mile from their current position. She quickly inputs the coordinates into the small hand-held teleportation box she did not return to Wu-Killers, Inc.

"The coordinates are locked in. We should teleport within a hundred feet radius of our target."

"What?" Rok practically shouts.

"Teleport? I'm not Captain Kirk and you sure

don't look like Scotty!"

She suddenly throws her body around him and presses a button on the transportation box in her hand.

"Here we go!" she giggles. They teleport and vanish from inside the parked van.

CHAPTER FIFTEEN

IN THE THROES OF EVIL

Their journey lasts but a single second. They materialize in a corridor of an office floor but one level above Da Man's current location. Their sudden appearance startles Judge Whitely who is strolling a few feet away at that very moment.

"How'd you get in here? Where'd you come from?" he stammers while reaching inside his coat to withdraw his gun.

Looking fierce and formidable, Anna already has her cannon-sized automatic aimed at the corpulent adjudicator.

"Don't even think about it, fatty!"

Rok glares at her. "He's not Da Man?"

"Not even close. But he *is* the closest thing to Da Man. He's the judge for half the eastern coast. He oversees all the free thought and creativity cases that come in and does Da Man's judicial dirty work. Judge Whitely is his name."

Whitely tries to sneak his right hand into his side coat pocket, but Anna steps toward him and uses her automatic to knock his hand away.

"Stand still and keep your hands behind your head!" She orders while aiming her automag at his face.

"This wonderful weapon is loaded with 2500 magnum explosive shells. They're designed to destroy artillery, automobiles, and armored vehicles. Imagine what it will do to your head at point blank range," she smiles wickedly.

"Look, I'm just Da Man's servant, one of many forced to do his bidding and follow orders. Down the hall, there is an elevator that will take you to his sanctuary. He's there now, only one floor below us."

Rok is annoyed by the look of Whitely, and steps towards him hastily.

"A servant, huh? Forced to take orders, huh? Just a poor, innocent judge just trying to survive, right," Rok chides while waving his own formidable weapon in Whitely's face.

Suddenly, Anna lashes out and hits the judge alongside the head, knocking him off his feet and to the floor unconscious.

"Hey!" scolds Rok, "I was going to do that. I just had a few more things to get off my chest, that's all. Woman, can't you let a guy have some fun, too?"

"Sorry babe, but we have no time for fun," she answers in a no-nonsense, practical tone.

"I must get to Da Man. You stay here and keep your eye on things so I can return to this level without any problems. It's much easier to teleport back to the same location from which you arrived. I need to make sure I can return to this level."

"Well, I can't let you take on Da Man alone."

"You have to. We need to maintain this escape route. It's our only option for exiting this location. Besides, I am Nzinga 5000, the most dangerous assassin in all the world. Da Man, my dear, will soon be Da Dead Pig!"

Saying that, she leans over and gives Rok a quick peck on the lips, then turns and hurries towards the elevator at the end of the hall. Rok follows her and enters the elevator right behind her. But she quickly pushes him out, back into the corridor. She smiles a friendly farewell to him as the lift's door quickly closes.

Inside the elevator, she pushes the button for the next floor, not knowing that the retina scanner needs to be accessed before anyone can control the elevator's actions. Instantly, a knockout gas is released into the elevator, and unfortunately, Anna inhales a few breaths before finding her portable gas mask and placing it over her nose and mouth. She immediately becomes groggy and has difficulty standing but is able to maintain consciousness. She's ready for this, having undergone gas chamber training in the past. The elevator jerks violently up and down, causing Anna to be slammed from side to side, rendering her more defenseless for the confrontation with Da Man that is only seconds away.

One floor below her Da Man stands watching a monitor which streams from a camera hidden on the elevator. Manipulating command buttons below the monitor, Da Man facilitated the release of the knockout gas and caused the chamber to thrash in the elevator shaft. Now he punches another button and the lift suddenly drops weightlessly. A millisecond later, it comes to a violent grinding halt which knocks Anna senselessly to the floor.

Da Man wastes no time. The doors open and he immediately begins firing his tri-barrel machinegun to saturate the elevator and its occupant with rounds of lead and steel. But Anna manages to scurry out the contraption on her belly, and while doing so, returns fire in Da Man's general direction. But she is hit several times during her exit from the lift. Tired expressions contorting her face clearly betray that things have not gone as planned.

Upstairs, Rok hears the battle ensuing below him. He repeatedly hits the elevator button to get it to return to his floor. Through the crack in the elevator doors he screams down to her.

"Anna, send the elevator back up for me! Hurry!"

"Can't babe. Can't reach it!" She gazes through the obstruction of furnishings and sees Da Man on the floor across from a mirror, rubbing his neck where one of her bullets hit him. But his skin looks like metal, and the wound on his neck is but a metallic scrape! She can't believe her eyes. The rumors are true. Da Man is part human, and part machine and computer, sporting a hide of cold, impermeable metallic skin.

From his location, Da Man gazes into the wide floor mirror across from him and sees Anna glaring at him. Re-gripping the huge machinegun in his heavy, metallic hands, he suddenly lunges to his feet and fires the weapon at full auto while he slowly and confidently, walks menacingly towards her. She jumps to her feet, too, and decides to meet him in this "head-to-head" confrontation. But a look of resignation lines her face. She knows this is a battle she cannot survive. Still, she realizes, it's one she doesn't have to lose.

"You're done now, bitch!" Da Man screams as he continues his assault.

"You dare think you could take me out all by yourself? Fool! Now die!"

More of Da Man's rounds hit her, and she is bleeding from her wounds, barely able to stand, she summons all her strength to continue her walk towards him. Her shooting arm hangs at her side, and the huge .50 caliber automag falls from her grasp. Desperately, she looks up at the ceiling above her and screams, "I love you Rok! I love you, forever!"

At that moment, Da Man is almost upon her and begins firing point-blank into her stomach and chest. To his surprise, she doesn't stop or fall to the floor, but in a last burst of strength and energy she lunges toward him, her arms flung wide in an all-out embrace. She savagely utters, to the evil cyborg, "Kill me, you ugly muthaf—! And kill yourself!"

Above them, Rok pounds on the elevator doors in desperation. A loud, forceful explosion erupts from below. In the same moment, Rok screams out, knowing full well the explosion's cause. He is flung backward from the elevator doors onto the floor, dazed and emotionally unnerved. His eyes fill with tears and his mouth trembles with rage. Yes, he knows what caused the explosion below him. He knows that the love of his life, Anna LaRue aka Agent Nzinga 500, has just given her life to save creativity.

CHAPTER SIXTEEN

THE SOLUTION

D ays and then weeks pass and we find Rok, Pooky, and Billis back at the estate, still mourning Anna's death, but honoring her life. They sit in Billis' living room watching old reruns of the old Time Tunnel television series from the 1990s. The atmosphere is subdued, but not entirely cheerless.

"You know Rok, when you time-traveled here, and after researching how it happened, you gave me the missing link to something I've being searching for, for a long time. You guys, come follow me," Billis says.

Turning off the 3D viewing screen, the two younger men follow him to a locked room located in the deep recesses of the estate. It is a room even Pooky never had access to.

"Wow Dad, what's this?"

"Well, while you've been hanging out with the

robots, managing the farm during the daytime for the last few years, I've been building this machine."

He unlocks the door, flips a switch, and the room is flooded with light. He motions for them to follow him inside. "The thing is, I've been working on a time traveling machine of my own."

Rok can't believe his eyes. "What? You mean this is gonna to me get back to where I came from?"

"Yes, that's my hope," Billis answers. "You see, I couldn't figure it out before, but now I understand. The energy created in that weather storm is the same amount of energy needed to make my machine operate.

"Wow, look at this thing!" Pooky exclaims. He and Rok examine with wide eyes the sophisticated, automobile-like, mechanical wonder sitting in the center of the room.

"My machine separates molecules to pass through a tiny subspace wormhole which I'm able to access with a current of integrated cosmic rays so all solid matter is disassembled and then reassembled after passing through the time displacement vortex."

"You say what?" Rok perplexedly asks. But then shakes his head.

"Never mind. Music's my thing, not science," he quips.

"I'm able to program this device to almost any time and location. Placement location would be essentially the same between time portals. However, I have finally discovered why I've been unable to transport anything larger than a jar of peanut butter. I've never had enough power to properly activate the Spinulator so that it can turn fast enough to separate a larger quantity of molecules."

"Dad, how come you didn't tell me about this before?" asks Pooky.

"I've learned that one shouldn't say much about a new invention until it's been completely invented. Plus, I didn't want you to accidentally let any of your friends know about what I've been working on. If Da Man got wind of it and got his hands on my machine, the world would really be in trouble. Past and future."

"So Billis, do you think your time machine will work?" Rok inquires in a serious voice. "I mean, I'm thinking now instead of me returning to my time, we could go back only a few weeks and save Anna and get rid of Da Man some other way."

Billis smiles at him, pleased of the fact that Rok has so quickly thought of this use for his time machine in lieu of the obvious suggestion of immediately returning him to 2010.

"But the thing is," Pooky suddenly thinks to add, "when will there be another big storm? And when it happens, how do we capture its power?"

"I have an answer to that. It's Rok's original storm that brought him here that made me think of it. It's simple. I figure with enough solar powered generators, I can produce sufficient energy that will mimic the storm that brought Rok here. Yes, I believe it could work, and yes, we could go back and try to save Anna. I have enough solar powered generators to get the job done."

"Whoa!" Pooky suddenly howls. "We could go back and eliminate Da Man before he comes to power, or even stop him from being born! We could even go back to help Shaka Zulu defeat the British. Or stop the slave trade. No! I got it, let's go way, way back and cut down that tree that Adam and Eve ate from. That was the start of all our problems!" Pooky excitedly continues. "Not that it matters cause we're only able to learn what 'The Man' wants us to know."

"Well," Billis hesitantly begins, "I wish we could do everything to improve everyone's life, and to guarantee that every human being would be created equal and have the same amount of happiness and success. I wish there weren't such things as lower and middle class and everyone was fortunate to live in abundance. Yeah, I wish we all could enjoy peace and utopia.

"Yeah, wouldn't that be something," Rok ponders.

"But it doesn't matter. I know now that my machine can only transport a person during the time in which he lives and has been alive. I cannot transport anyone one second before or after his lifespan. But yes, I would love to screw with time and play God, I guess. Possibly go back and eliminate every despicable murderer and terrorist and tyrant our world has ever known. Save all the people whose lives were cut down too soon. Hell, maybe even find out how Da Man became who and what he was."

"Hey, I hear you," Rok commiserates.

"But my machine can only do so much and go so far. I suspect we are very lucky that God granted us such a limitation," Billis whispers.

"But still Pops, there's one thing we're not limited from doing. We could go back and save mom from that car crash!"

"Well, Pooky, that's really what mainly inspired me to attempt to build this contraption in the first place. Too often I have imagined if I could have been with her, I could have made the autocar swerve and miss that hydrobus. Her life would have been saved and she'd be with us now," Billis' voice trails off almost to a whisper.

"So that's what happened to your mom, Pooky? Rok asks. "I'm so sorry for your loss. But hey, let's see if we can get this thing working. Let's do it!"

"Yes, let's do," Billis says, wiping a tear from his eye and hugging his son.

The next few days find our trio of musicians-turned-scientists busy getting Billis' time machine connected to the solar-powered generators and up and running and operational. Finally, with the machine completely ready for use, its sensitive controls expertly calibrated, Billis shows Pooky and Rok how to input the time and location stamp so the time traveler can be safely transported to the correct temporal and physical location. Fortunately, Billis has found a way to program the machine to accept physical placement within a fifty-mile radius and to do so with pin-point accuracy.

In this case, for the time traveling trip at hand, the accuracy needed *is* pin point. The plan is to place Rok inside the van with Anna just before the two of them teleport inside the White House to confront Da Man. The day and moment of reckoning arrives, and Rok finds himself attired just as he was that fateful night when he was with Anna in the van. Rok enters the time machine and secures himself comfortably inside. Billis explains to him that he might experience some tingling along the surface of his body and moments of dizziness before arriving at his destination.

Before closing the chamber door, he gives Rok a hug.

"If I ever wanted another son, it would be you," he says to Rok.

A moment later, Pooky reaches inside to hug him, too. Then the windowless door is closed and automatically locks and seals. Billis and his son position themselves in an enclosed cubical in front of the machine where Rok can view them through the front plexiglass window. Rok can read their lips when both say good luck to him. Then, the machine rumbles to life with flashing lights and loud vibrating sounds, the Spinulator roars to action and the time traveling process starts.

Suddenly, the light inside the capsule becomes unbearable, and Rok clinches his eyes shut and grinds his teeth to help endure this final stage of the transportation process.

From behind their protective cubical, wearing heavy, protective goggles, Billis and Pooky watch as an eerie light creates an aura around the time machine, reaching a blinding brightness. Then, it and its passenger instantly vanish from their sight.

EPILOGUE

The last thing Rok remembers is Billis and Pooky fading from view, then shutting his eyes to withstand the brilliant light and billowing vibrations. But now, the whole event seems surreal and like a dream. For he finds himself strapped to a medical gurney, flat on his back and looking up at what appears to be the ceiling of a helicopter! He can feel its vibrations and knows he's in flight. The wind against his face and a host of palpable sensations prove this must be the case.

"What the—" he exclaims, feeling the dryness of his throat. "How did the helicopter...wait, what's going on? How'd I get here? Did it lose power when the lightning struck us? That's what I thought, but I was only half-conscious. The details are still a little fuzzy."

EMT Jackson is leaning over him and smiling. Wearing a headset, he speaks in excited tones to the three other people inside the aircraft tuned in to his radio frequency.

"Hey guys, he's waking up. I don't believe it!"

Nearby, with a glowing wide grin spread across her face, Nurse LaRue echoes Jackson's ecstatic affirmation.

"Yes, it's true. He is regaining consciousness!"

"What do you mean he's waking up," the pilot exclaims.

"Yes sir, our patient is now fully awake!" Jackson answers.

Rok blinks several times as he opens his eyes and weakly smiles at Nurse LaRue through the translucent oxygen mask draped over his nose and mouth. She quickly but gently removes it, and warmly smiles down at him.

"It's a miracle. That's what it is, gentlemen," she announces.

Rok coughs a few times after the mask is removed, then feels a sudden pang in his heart, remembering Billis and Pooky. He's missing them already! Though barely able to speak, he finds himself full of questions.

"Hey, why am I strapped down like this? What's going on? Where are we? Hmmm, you look familiar."

He blinks again as he recognizes each detail of her

face. She's the splitting image of Nzinga 5000, his soulmate Anna from 2083!

"Nurse LaRue, let's allow him to sit up if he wants to," Jackson says to her. She adeptly begins to loosen his straps.

"Nurse LaRue?" he inquires, now gazing at her. "Your first name wouldn't be Anna, would it?"

She returns his strange glare and answers, "Yes it is. How'd you know that?"

"Oh, just a hunch. That's all. Just a hunch."

For a moment, he leans up and gazes out of the window directly across from him, then falls back on the gurney with exhaustion. He has flashbacks of the future, which strangely now seem like the past. He remembers the last month of his life. Crawling away from the wrecked helicopter, meeting Pooky and then Billis, learning about Da Man, meeting Anna, making love to her and falling in love with her. He remembers the explosion and her dying just one floor beneath him along with Da Man. Where are the vineyards? The giant grapes? Billis' expansive estate? Pooky's 3D watch? Anna's warm embrace and soft lips? The time machine?

As they fly through the end of the tumultuous storm, "How did he come out of that coma?" is the question on everyone's mind.

"This is monumental you guys! I can't believe it," Nurse LaRue claims.

The copilot theorizes to the others, "I wonder if when the lightning struck the helicopter, the electricity somehow passed through the aircraft and into him and caused him to awaken from his coma? You know, like a mega-defibrillator! Isn't his gurney metallic?"

Yes, Rok answers to himself. *Metallic, like the skin and soul of Da Man.* But was it all a dream? Was any of it real? *Wow*, he suddenly ponders, *what if I can foresee the future? What if creativity becomes completely regulated?*

"Well, we'll probably fly right back to the hospital after we land at the clinic," the pilot says. "He doesn't need any special treatment now."

Rok stares at the four crew members but is seeing beyond them. What if years from now, Da Man comes along and makes creativity illegal and enslaves the entire human race? What if all bird life dies due to man's destruction of the environment? What if incarcerated minorities and the disenfranchised have their DNA cloned to provide some kind of new slave work force? Worse yet, what if minorities lose their identities altogether? What happens with the loss of community power? What if he never gets to hear The Funk Sonatra Project ever again? Suddenly, a smile creases his face.

"His vitals are very good. He's even smiling," Nurse LaRue informs everyone.

"Who wouldn't, Anna, after laying eyes on you," Jackson laughs.

Rok looks up at her and returns her smile and quietly asks, "In my bag there, inside should be my shades. Can you get 'em for me, Anna, please? We've got ourselves a lot of things we need to change in this here world and it's important I have my shades and am looking and feeling as ultimately cool as possible!"

"What?" she says, a confused expression on her face.

"Oh, never mind. I'll tell you later. Once I'm back on the ground, got my shades on, and I've had time to chat with Frank. But the first thing we're going to do is take a drag around the track while I play a funky version of *Come Fly With Me*. Then we'll get to saving the world, babe," Rok laughs.

ABOUT THE AUTHOR

A fitness gym owner for almost a decade, **O.W. Serellus** is a controversial figure that often finds himself debating with others about the necessity of creativity without widespread control. In music, he believes thoughtful song writing and high-quality instrumentation are the minimum requirements for masterful artistry. O.W. enjoys spending time with his family, exercising, analyzing contact sports, admiring classic cars, and producing music. He resides in the San Francisco Bay Area and *The Funk Sonatra Project* is his first published book.

AN INTERVIEW WITH THE AUTHOR

The Funk Sonatra Project is based on a unique storyline. Where did the idea come from?

The idea of having wars waged over creativity instead of oil, land, or material possessions isn't farfetched. The idea of entire nations fighting and slaughtering each other, not in the name of love or God or religion, but for the right to think and create or control those who do—isn't farfetched either. Imagine a world where such activity is a curse to tyrants and dictators everywhere. A realm where creativity is to be stifled or harbored or outright destroyed. If there is an entity (or deity) who controls the source or power of creativity, we can all imagine a universe where that, as well as the exercise of creativity, is deemed more threatening than freedom of speech or worship, or even life itself. I've always questioned that. Why does it seem that creativity is controlled?

What do you want readers to walk away thinking after reading The Funk Sonatra Project?

A politically incorrect but accurately possible vision of what the not-so-distant future holds for Earth and all individuals whose passion and vocation is one of creativity. I want readers to experience a provocative tale rife with suspense, mystery, and intrigue, concerning other individuals whose passion and sole purpose is to control, destroy, or utterly prevent freedom of creativity.

Why do you believe people need to read books like this one?

To cause them to question their own creative thoughts and beliefs. But at the same time, understand what motivates artistic individuals everywhere to remain independent and loyal to what their minds think and create, to keep their works and creative endeavors sacred and secure, while knowing such inimitable value cannot and must not be sold for mere profit or gain.

Which character was your favorite and which was the most challenging to write and develop?

Unfortunately, there isn't a favorite character, although Da Man is the most disliked. Writing Nzinga was a challenge. I wanted to describe her upbringing and her training in detail to give the readers an idea of how much she endured to be one of the world's best assassins and not just focus on her mesmerizing beauty. She's an important link to the story, which is why the reader will be sad at the end, but to be continued…

What do you see in the future for The Funk Sonatra Project?

It will irrevocably alter the thoughts and creativity of even the most unpersuaded of minds. I aim to provide an opinionated and cogent answer to many cosmic questions. But especially it dares to answer, "What if?" and "Why is that?"

You offer this innovative story along with a listening soundtrack, correct?

Yes, there is a soundtrack which was created to complement the novel. Two of the characters in the story produced it and it is appropriately titled, *The Funk Sonatra Project.*

A Special Thanks from O.W. Serellus

To my lovely wife, Jo Williams, who has been an extraordinary support system for me, and I am truly a fortunate man. She put her dreams on hold to help with mine. My only goal is to swing for the fences with ventures so the result can be an early retirement for her. She spoiled me while I was dreaming and creating ways of becoming financially free. While she would simply refer to her actions as love, I see them for far more—an absolute blessing. *I'm extremely thankful to you for your help in all that you do from spiritual love, emotional love, and physical love.* You birthed and mothered our daughters and they are a special gift from GOD. I thank The Almighty for putting you in my life. Babe, you are the ultimate woman and the love of my life!

Also, I must acknowledge and send a big *I love you* to our three daughters, Mahal, Fela, Najah. Remember, aim to be spiritual in your everyday walk and pray daily. Stick to Ed (your education) until you have all you need to be on your own two feet.

To my pillars, my Mom and Dad, thank you for your unconditional love and undeniable support! Thank you for your creativity and entrepreneurial spirit.

To my big brother, the best big brother, thank you for being the best. I love you all and will continue to aim to do positive work.

Also, a special thanks to my remaining family members and dearest friends.

Peace!